AUTHOR'S NOTE

Dear Reader,

I've been writing for decades, but I started writing romantic stories around 2010, when I wanted to share a romantic event in my life with my readers. Yes, most of the stories are based on real-life events from my life or close friends and relatives. I have added a little of my imagination to make the stories more exciting (fictional).

In this book, you will find stories that are highly romantic, sensuous and innovative from a sisterhood of women living life. Some of my stories are super sexy with high drama and high emotion, while others are the love-me-tender with plenty of affection and romance. No matter what kind of romance you like—I think you will find an enjoyable story in my writing.

I hope you enjoy these captivating stories!

Cheryl Holloway

WHAT READERS ARE SAYING ABOUT
A SISTERHOOD OF WOMEN LIVING LIFE!

FIVE STARS! "Cheryl Holloway has created real stories about real women living real life and life isn't always fair, but it is REAL."

FIVE STARS! "I can certainly relate to some of these stories and some of these women."

FIVE STARS! "Cheryl's short stories offer lessons learned by women of all ages."

FIVE STARS! "These stories make you realize that you see women every day and you have no idea what their journey is all about."

FIVE STARS! "Cheryl Holloway's stories make you smile, cry and laugh—just like life. I love her writing style."

FIVE STARS! "I enjoyed the book so much that I bought it as a gift for my mom, sisters, and my BFF."

FIVE STARS! "This is awesome, a must read!"

ALSO BY CHERYL HOLLOWAY

Cougar Tales series

Father and Son (Book 1)
Italian Basketball Player (Book 2)
Jamaican Love (Book 3)
Cougar Tales Box Set: Books 1-3

Other

The Bane Bath Salts (A drug prevention fiction eBook for Young Adults/Teens)

The Proposal: A Leap of Faith (Short Story)

For previews of upcoming books and short stories by Cheryl Holloway and more information about the author, visit www.CherylHolloway.net.

For free books and the "Reader Loyalty Bonus" visit www.CherylHollowaybooks.wordpress.com.

Connect with Me

I love hearing from you—so please don't be shy! Email me (authorCherylHolloway@gmail.com), if you would like to be notified when new books have been released; or to be informed of free or discounted prices and promotions; or to receive exclusive excerpts and freebies. Or please sign up for my blog and get a free Cheryl Holloway eBook too!

A Sisterhood of Women Living Life

The Short Story Collection Book 1

Cheryl Holloway

Holloway House

ISBN-13 (print): 978-0-692-93096-0
Library of Congress Control Number: 2017951886

Publisher's Note: This book is a work of fiction. Names, characters, places and incidents are either the product of the author's imagination or are used fictitiously. Any resemblance to actual persons, living or dead, or to actual events or locales is entirely coincidental.

Cover and Logo Design by: John E. Smith
Smith's Choice Graphics

Print Formatting: By Your Side Self-Publishing
www.ByYourSideSelfPub.com

First: Holloway House printing, August 2017
Printed in U.S.A.

Adult reading material

PUBLISHED BY:

Holloway House
1282 Smallwood Drive West, Suite 116
Waldorf, MD 20603-4732
1-877-974-8318

DEDICATION

Dedicated to the Loving Memory of my Daughter

~Nichelle Lorraine Robinson King~

ACKNOWLEDGMENTS

As always, I thank the Lord for blessing me with the ability to write and for always being by my side.

I was sustained every single day by the love and support of my friends and family.

A special thanks to all of the people who helped me with the edits, formatting, research, ideas, interviews, revisions and general information.

A special thanks to my beta readers—I couldn't do it without you—Kenyan Smith, Paula Mitchell, Mary Whyte, and Geri Smith.

A special thanks to all of the ladies in the Accokeek Women's Writing Group, who helped with suggestions and comments.

A special thanks to Georgette Littlejohn, the writer who I mentored and helped to become an author in a short amount of time.

Thank you to all of you who were not mentioned by name. I know who you are and that means the world to me.

Thanks to my readers and supporters—each one of you is very special and extremely important!

Also… a very special thanks to anyone who writes a review on Amazon or Goodreads.

CONTENTS

Short Stories

A Sisterhood of Women Living Life

The Dreaded After Call

The Dreaded After Call

The last three hours have been grueling for the entire staff while going over the bluelines—the final copy before print. Especially, since today we had a pre-dawn start for the latest issue of the *Sacramento Metropolitan* magazine. Dy'Anne Harrell, the thirty-seven year old Editor, the first African American to head a magazine of this circulation size, took this job a few months ago and this was the first issue under her complete supervision. For her own safety net, she grabs it and holds herself hostage while she double checks it one last time. She has to prove to the powers-that-be that yes, a woman can hold the reigns of a magazine this size, and she can hold them tight!

But for the last ten minutes, she's looked at the same word on the same page several times and for some reason, she just can't move her eyes to the next page. It's scary— she feels as if something will drastically change things. Finally, she closes her eyes, puts both hands on her forehead and decides to rest her mind and eyes—if only for a few seconds. This will surely provide clear thinking for her. But suddenly her foot starts moving nervously. *The stress is mounting. I... am... in... charge!*

The phone's loud inter-office buzzer startled Dy'Anne. She immediately glanced at the gold clock shaped like a book on her desk, a going-away gift from the magazine that she just left. *It's 9:03.* She thought to herself, *Ump, the Army doesn't have anything on me, I can do just as much, if not more, than they can before 9:00 a.m.*

The phone buzzed again. And she yelled at the closed door, "Avril, I said NO calls, as in none, nada, zip! I'm busy, remember!"

All Avril DuPree, her administrative assistant, could get out of her mouth was, "I know, but…"

The door opened before Dy'Anne retorted with, "Have you lost your mind? I'm still going over the bluelines!"

Opening the door to Dy'Anne's office and poking her head in, Avril pleaded, "I know, Dy'Anne, but there's some guy on the phone who refuses to hang up until he speaks to you. He said that he's called every office of the McKnight Publishing Company on the West Coast, and now that he's found you, he will not hang up until he talks to you… personally. Dy'Anne, I hung up on him twice, because I thought it was a prank call, but he keeps calling back!"

"Who the Hell does he think he is? I said no calls. Just tell him that I am not taking any calls at the moment. Get rid of him, Avril. Pretty please."

Avril walked away mumbling in her native New Orleans' French shaking her head, as she closed the door behind her.

Dy'Anne continued proofing and about halfway down the page, Avril gently knocked on the door—again.

"Dy'Anne, he said that it's an emergency."

"Okay. Who is this guy with the e-mer-gen-cy?"

"Noel Rogers."

"Who… Whooo did you say?" Dy'Anne stammered.

"He said that his name is Noel Rogers."

Dy'Anne's hesitation waned after just a moment. There was a long, long silence. All Dy'Anne could hear was the clock ticking—for what seemed to be forever.

Judging from the distressed look on Dy'Anne's face, Avril frantically said, "Are you all right? Do you need me to get you a glass of water? You look like you just saw a ghost from the N'Orleans Cemetery."

The present had already erased most of the past... but his call made so many memories return.

"Uh, Uh. I mean... Yes, I'm Okay." Regaining her composure, Dy'Anne continued, "Uh, Avril, please tell him that I'm busy in your most convincing voice. Uh, get his number and tell him that I **will** call him back, later today."

"Okay. But this guy is persistent!"

"Yes, I know. He is very persistent, and Noel **always** gets what Noel wants..." As Dy'Anne's voice trailed away to the past, the memories suddenly flooded her mind—causing her both unexpected pleasure and undeniable pain.

Dy'Anne stared out her window—not looking at the trees, or the people, or the scenery—not really looking at anything, just thinking about Noel Rogers. Remembering the tall—six foot five inch—medium build, distinguished looking gentleman. His curly, jet-black hair was beginning to slightly gray around the temples, but in a sophisticated kind-of-way. He had the cutest upturned lips when he smiled—somehow you always wanted to give him a sloppy, puppy-dog kiss and knock his glasses askew in the process. He had a beautiful I-just-got-off-the-beach tan. And his butt; it was the kind that you wanted to squeeze with both hands and it just turned her on so much—that she had given him a gold chain with a charm that read "cute ass." She smiled just as a tear slid down her face. How she wished she could stop the flood of memories— of love. But she just couldn't stop it. So many thoughts were penetrating her mind, so fast.

She sighed and continued her thoughts. *He should be forty-five years old, now. I haven't seen or heard from him since that day. Hmmm... it's been almost a year—one very long and extremely tormenting time of trying to forget him. Forget the love of my life. Forget that we were soul mates. Forget that we had been dating for two years. Forget that we were engaged. Forget the moment I found out that he was still legally married. Forget what he said. Forget that he couldn't divorce his wife, because of the humiliation she had caused him when she left him for a woman. Forget his stupid reasoning. Forget that he loved me unconditionally. And... forgive myself for being such a fool!*

As quick as a flash of lightning, Dy'Anne's pleasant thoughts of Noel changed to angry thoughts. *She remembered! Hell, yes, she remembered the frustration of that last fretful day. The heated argument they had—on their last day together as a couple. It was carved in her mind. Damn. She hurriedly left for California without giving him her new address or phone number—only the name of her new publishing company. How could true love end in such a tragedy?*

Dy'Anne had been so preoccupied with thoughts of the past that she did not notice Avril still standing in the doorway. She was shocked back to reality by the sound of Avril's voice.

"Dy'Anne, he's still on hold."

Startled, she stopped staring out the window and abruptly turned around.

"What?"

"Dy'Anne, are you Okay? You have tears streaming down your face!" Avril said with concern in her voice and heart.

Dy'Anne was embarrassed to let Avril see her in this state of mind. She had always been so professional, never letting anyone at the office see even a peak into her personal life. She was always a very private person—that is until now. She had always cleverly hidden her emotions—even when her father, Gordon Harrell, died. He was Dy'Anne's best friend. She had faithfully talked to him every day for the last fifteen years, since his first heart attack, before the Pacemaker. She believed that their talks were what kept him alive all that time—the mere fact that "daddy's little girl needed him." Dy'Anne was frustrated that the two men, who she loved the most in the whole world were no longer in her life—one by his choice and one by God's choice. She loved and needed them both.

Why, God?

She thought about her beloved daddy. Just last winter, when she had a flat tire in San Francisco, he confirmed what she already knew when she called him long distance to ask what to do about a flat tire, and he told her to "call Triple A." But things seemed so much more "official," when it was labeled as "advice from her daddy." No one had ever pampered her like her daddy—no one except Noel. Not even her mom, "the wicked witch of the East." She couldn't think about her daddy without thinking about her mom. It was the positive and the negative—the electrical polarity. Somehow her and her mom never got along. They just argued, and argued, and argued some more. Having children had ruined her mom's career as a ballerina. She was elated to get all of her childbearing days over in one attempt when she had the perfect set of twins—a boy and a girl. But life turned to unhappiness when Ryan remained ill with some rare disease from the day of his birth until the day of his death at three years old. Dy'Anne still never grew up with a mother, because her mom blamed herself for her child's sickness; and ultimately, she spent a lifetime mourning for her baby boy—and ignoring her baby girl.

So, Dy'Anne grew up only having her father to talk to and confide in. Their closeness was what she needed and lived for. And when her father died, a part of Dy'Anne died, too. The difference between her and her mother was that Dy'Anne hadn't given up on life when someone she loved died. But she still hadn't shed one tear in the office when she returned to work a month after her daddy's funeral.

And now, here she was crying a truckload of tears over just the thought of talking to Noel. And in front of Avril!

Embarrassed, she grabbed four tissues, wiped her eyes and blew her nose. Dy'Anne was confused and her whole life flashed before her eyes.

"Avril, really I am just fine," she said as she tried to convince Avril, as well as herself. "Please, give me a moment alone... and I'll be fine."

Avril quickly left Dy'Anne's office and just as she reached her desk, a delivery guy entered the outer office carrying flowers. He was excited and asked her to sign, date and time the delivery. He was going to get a one hundred dollar tip, if it had been delivered in thirty minutes or less.

Dy'Anne knew that she had to pull herself together before Avril came back and she could not let her emotions get the best of her. Yes, she loved Noel so much, but he had performed the worst sin—he had broken her heart and her trust. She straightened her silk blouse, looked in the mirror and finger brushed her hair—as if she were going to see Noel in person.

Avril returned shortly and said, "These flowers were just delivered. Do you want to see the card? And Mr. Rogers is still holding."

"No. I know who sent them, just by looking at the arrangement—two dozen purple roses and a single white calla lily in the middle. It's from Noel. But just out of curiosity, what does the card say?"

"It says, 'I miss you and now that I've finally found you, I will never let you go!' But it's not signed."

"I'll talk to him... uh, just to clear up the phone line."

"Yeah, right!" Avril said sarcastically.

Dy'Anne didn't know what she was going to say. She just knew that life was too short to deal with a married man.

Dy'Anne took one long, deep breath to give herself the extra strength and courage to deal with the unexpected... Noel. She knew that she still loved him and that he would always be the love of her life. She believed that they were soul mates. She knew that deep down in the crevices of her heart and the dark, dusty corners of her mind, her love for Noel would remain until the day that she drew her last breath. But she had to be strong, and she had to do the right thing, or surely he would draw her back into his web of deceit… unintentionally. Her faith in God would not allow her to date a married man—under no circumstances.

She closed her eyes and quickly prayed a silent prayer: *Dear God, It's me, Dy'Anne. I'm currently on an emotional roller coaster. Please, don't let my mind follow my heart—unless it's Your will. Amen.*

Silent tears streamed down her cheeks and in her coldest business voice destined for any old stranger, surely not for the love of her life, Dy'Anne said, "Hello, Mr. Rogers. This is Dy'Anne Harrell. How may I help you?"

"Dy'Anne, I'm so glad to finally talk to you. I have something very important to tell you," Noel said with a sense of urgency.

"Yes, I'm listening," she said in her proper uninterested voice.

"I love you. I'm divorced, and I want to marry you!"

Dy'Anne was speechless and couldn't say anything for what seemed like an eternity.

"Dy'Anne… Dy'Anne, are you still there?" Noel said with desperation.

"Yes, I am," Dy'Anne stammered. "Is this a proposal?"

"Sort of, but I would like to do it properly, if you will allow me. I've been carrying around your engagement ring for months. Dy'Anne, the waiting period is over. Let's meet tonight for dinner and for our formal proposal to be married on the day of your choice."

"Yes, I'd like that, and Noel… I love you!"

THE END

A Sisterhood of Women Living Life:

Wine A Little or A Little Wine

Wine a Little or a Little Wine

Chapter One

Jaclyn waited a few more minutes for her blind date to show up at the Crestview Bar and Grill. He was already an hour late—maybe there was a lot of traffic. She sat at the bar nursing a cosmopolitan. She looked up at the door as a stranger entered. He walked over to the bartender and asked for a shot. He hurriedly drank it down, as though he was about to be executed.

He was only a few feet from Jaclyn and she could hear their conversation.

"I'm supposed to be meeting a blind date here this evening. Have you seen any ugly chicks hanging around?" the stranger asked.

"No, just a couple of nice looking ladies who are regulars."

"Really. Maybe my luck has changed."

"Possibly," the bartender said and went to get another customer a drink.

The stranger looked around and smiled at Jaclyn. He got off the barstool and walked over to the skinny blonde.

They talked for a few minutes and then he left her and walked up to the brunette wearing stilettos. They exchanged words and he came back to the bar.

"Well, maybe she left, cause I don't think it's the chubby chick on my left," he told the bartender.

Jaclyn had about a half of a drink left. She calmly got up, took her drink with her, walked up to the stranger and said, "I guess your blind date was with the chubby chick, but I'm too good for you!" And with that Jaclyn threw her remaining drink in his face, turned, and left the bar.

Jaclyn was a full-figured young woman with a "pretty face," as everyone always told her. She had just finished her MBA in Education and had recently received a promotion on her six-figure job at the Department of Education. Jaclyn considered herself to be an eligible single woman, but didn't understand why she couldn't find a decent guy to date, and she definitely would not sink to dating someone like the stupid stranger.

She drove her BMW home to her new condo, where she went into her bedroom and looked into the mirror and vowed to give up men—period. All she wanted to do was wine a little. She would not be a lesbian, but she would not date any more assholes like the stranger. She would live her life and be the best person she could be, and if her soul mate was out there in the universe, he could find her!

Six Months Later

Jaclyn had a rough day at work and things were just going downhill faster than a snowball in an avalanche. Her boss had given her a new project that she just didn't seem to be able to get off the ground. Her vacation reservations were mysteriously canceled. Her best friend, Joyce, had just told her that she found the cutest bridesmaids dresses for the wedding in size seven and that she couldn't be a bride's maid because the dress didn't come in a size sixteen. Her mom called to tell her that she had a new man in her life—at fifty plus.

Jaclyn thought, *WTF!*

Jaclyn decided to go to Trader Joe's to get some steaks and peach coleslaw for dinner and TJ's key lime pie for dessert. She decided to pick up a bottle of wine to go with dinner. She was in the wine section when this tall, handsome guy kept looking at her.

He finally said something, "You look a bit confused. May I help you with the selection of a good wine?"

"And what makes you a wine connoisseur?" Jaclyn said sarcastically.

"I'm sorry. Let me introduce myself. I'm Bobby McArthur. I work at The Wine Specialist, the largest wine store in the area, and I have a wine show, *The Metro Wine Glass* on channel 28."

"Oh, my, you really are a wine connoisseur," she chortled.

"Yes, and I would love to help a beautiful lady pick out a good wine for her dinner party. You know the old saying, 'The best wines are the ones we drink with friends.' Don't you agree?"

"Yes, I agree. But I'm not having a dinner party. I had a rough day, and I just wanted to put a steak on the grill, have a baked potato and peach coleslaw, with key lime pie for dessert to pamper myself."

"A lady after my own heart. A good meal is great for pampering yourself. But why doesn't your husband or boyfriend pamper you?"

"No such luck. I don't have a significant other."

"Wow. Someone who is in the same boat as myself."

"Really? You should have women breaking down doors to have you in their life."

"I guess they forgot to send out the memo." And they both had a hearty laugh.

"Well, I don't want to keep you waiting. Let me make

a couple of suggestions and I will be out of your way. How about TJ's Petit Reserve? They have a Pinot Noir from California's Central Coast that is heavenly. They also have a Pinot Grigio from Monterey County. The grapes are estate grown, and you should sip it slowly to enjoy the flavor. Well, I don't want to out stay my welcome. I will see you around."

And Bobby McArthur was gone as quickly as he had appeared.

When he left, she wished that she had gotten his number.

She gathered both wines that he had suggested and headed for the register.

Just as she was about to leave the store, the manager walked up to her and handed her a package.

He said, "The gentleman left this for you. It is paid for, and he said that he was sure you would enjoy it."

"Thank you," Jaclyn took the package and opened it.

It was a bottle of Honey Moon Viognier with his business card attached, and a note on the back that read, 'This wine is great with salmon or shrimp. Call me and tell me what you think."

Bobby McArthur had just made Jaclyn Mason's day— a bright and sunny day!

Chapter Two

Jaclyn woke up this morning feeling like she owned the world. A few days had passed since she had met Bobby McArthur, and she thought *if I'm going to call him, this is the day*.

So, she mustered up enough nerve and nervously dialed his number.

He answered on the third ring.

"Hello. May I speak to Bobby McArthur?" Jaclyn nervously beamed.

"Yes, this is he. May I ask who's calling?"

"This is Jaclyn Mason. The lady you met in Trader Joe's and you suggested some wines for me to try."

"Well, hello, Jaclyn. I was wondering when you would try the Honey Moon Viognier and give me a call."

"I tried it with some shrimp kabobs and loved it. It was a very nice white wine."

"I knew you would like it. So, have your days been better than the last time I saw you?"

"Yes, they have been considerably better."

Jaclyn didn't quite know what to say to keep the conversation rolling, but Bobby kept it moving along smoothly.

They talked for over an hour, and then Bobby suggested that they meet the next day for lunch at a nice little mom and pop restaurant near Trader Joe's. Jaclyn agreed and when she got off the phone, she glowed like a light in the middle of the dark woods.

Bobby had picked a great restaurant off the beaten path with good service and an attentive staff. Jaclyn noticed that most of the tables were filled with locals who seemed to be eating their meals in a leisurely manner. It was a nice sunny day, so Bobby suggested that they eat on the patio where there were less people and they could enjoy a little privacy. He was right; they shared the area with only one other couple. The lunch was delicious and light, while the conversation was friendly and hearty. Jaclyn and Bobby's lunch date was excellent!

Over the next few weeks, they had enjoyed several compatible and friendly dates, which resulted in Bobby asking Jaclyn if she would mind if they could exclusively date each other. She was delighted and agreed.

This was certainly a turn for the better in both of their lives.

Her friend's wedding was coming up and now that they were "a couple," she decided to ask Bobby if he would like to accompany her to the event. He agreed and Jaclyn knew that she would be happy to show off her new man to her college friends, especially since she was no longer in the wedding party.

Her friend, Joyce, had a very special Victorian venue picked out with a local caterer; however, two days before the wedding, they found out it had been double booked and the venue was going to the other couple. Her friend's wedding was beginning to turn into a disaster, and the laughing stock of the wedding community, since all of the better places were booked solid. Joyce and her husband-to-be had to find a venue and a caterer, literally the day before the wedding.

So, Joyce with wedding jitters and frantic plans, asked her best friend for last-minute help. Jaclyn wanted to help Joyce, but kept thinking about how her friend had cut her out of the wedding because she was a size sixteen instead of size seven. *That was a hard pill to swallow, and they had been friends since their childhood.*

So… Jaclyn decided to forget what her friend had done, and help her friend in time of need. *After all, that's what friends do.*

Jaclyn and Bobby saved the day! Bobby got a Bed & Breakfast for the venue and he persuaded one of his colleagues to cater the event. Bobby used two ornate wine fountains from his show for a mini wine tasting of two very different wines. He persuaded another friend to provide a limousine service to transport guests to and from the venues. It was too short of notice for a big wedding cake, so they improvised with a dessert buffet for guests and a small wedding cake for the bride and groom.

The wedding, although planned at the last minute, turned out to be a success. Most of the guests didn't even know what happened until the wedding and reception were over.

Joyce realized that in a pinch, Jaclyn was a "true" friend and that she had been wrong in cutting her out of the bridal party. As a token of appreciation, Joyce made Jaclyn her maid of honor and she was allowed to wear the dress and color of her choice.

Jaclyn was grateful to Bobby for mending her friendship with Joyce and making her the best friend ever in Joyce's eyes. This gesture deepened and strengthened the relationship between Bobby and Jaclyn. It also created a wonderfully new bond between all of them.

A new friendship was born between the couples, and the four of them spent several weekends together.

Chapter Three

Jaclyn and Bobby were ecstatic that their life together was so fulfilling. They had some great times together, like the night they went to the movies. After the movie, Bobby was driving Jaclyn home when it started to rain. They waited in the car until the rain slacked off, but then it started raining harder again.

Bobby turned to Jaclyn and was about to ask her a question, when she said, "Do you want to run in the rain?" They both smiled and ran to her door, while getting soaked and laughing—together.

Jaclyn thought, *It's these kind of dates that make me feel special.*

It was the middle of the week, and it was not only a bad hair day, but Jaclyn was having a bad day at work. Bobby had called her to take her to lunch to try to cheer her up, but it just wasn't happening today with her boss' attitude. So, he told her that he would stop by for a few minutes after work with a bottle of wine.

At around 6 p.m., Bobby rang the bell and Jaclyn answered the door. He handed Jaclyn a wine bag that made her smile. It read, "Stolen from Santa's Wine Cellar." He gave her a kiss on the cheek and said, "I've got to run, but there's something special in the bag to cheer you up." She thanked him and closed the door.

When she opened the bag, there was a necklace wrapped around the bottle neck. There was a tiny diamond Eiffel Tower on the necklace. Jaclyn smiled because Bobby had remembered that she loved Paris. There was French wine in the bag also. She smiled from ear-to-ear and left him a nice message on his voice mail.

They shared quality time together on many occasions.

Dating life for them was good and getting better. Every day with Bobby was like a new adventure. It had been a very delightful year since the two had started dating.

The five-year anniversary for Bobby's Wine Show was quickly approaching and he was planning a special show. Jaclyn had been to his show several times and thought that it had "belle ambiance." But this was the first time that Joyce and her husband had been to the live show.

Jaclyn was becoming a wine connoisseur. She even had learned about the "tears of wine," near the top of a glass of wine. She was learning a lot from Bobby and his show.

Bobby was so excited about the upcoming event and wanted Jaclyn, Joyce, and her husband to join him on the show.

The show was fantastic and one to remember. Besides the regular critiques, top sommeliers were on hand to talk about all of the wine things and local chefs were demonstrating delicious appetizers and mouth-watering recipes for the audience to sample. Jaclyn thought that the show was always more enjoyable in person than watching it on the flat screen.

About three quarters of the way into the show, Bobby told his audience, "I have a very special guest here today that I would like to introduce to my world. Come on up on stage, Jaclyn… This is Jaclyn Mason, the love of my life."

At that moment, Bobby got down on one knee and stated, "Jaclyn, will you marry me?"

Jaclyn had a surprised look on her face and avowed, "Yes, Bobby, I will."

Bobby looked at Jaclyn and said, "You and wine, my two favorite things."

The audience cheered and gave Jaclyn and Bobby a standing ovation.

Bobby affirmed, "She said yes, folks, and that means wine and a souvenir glass for everyone to remember this day!"

THE END/THE BEGINNING

A Sisterhood of Women Living Life:

A Widow Moves On

A Widow Moves On

Chapter One

"Billy, love of my life and husband of my youthful dreams, I've mourned you far too long. I must move on— for my sanity," Katherine announced as she talked to the picture of her deceased husband.

Then she stood and looked herself directly in the face and divulged to her mirror image, "Yes, I loved him for twenty-six years, and I will always love him, but I'm still young and I know there is still room for joy and love in my life. Widowhood isn't easy. I have to bite the bullet and start dating, so that I can seriously move on."

Katherine thought about what she had learned at the Grief and Bereavement Support Group. She saw first-hand how others were coping with their loss, and she had learned to live with the loss. She wanted to heal her broken heart. She insisted out loud, "I am adjusting. I need to do this for me. I'm determined, and I will find a widowhood dating service. My fiftieth birthday is in two months. I'm not lucky enough to have had children. I ran into health problems that made it impossible. Billy was all that I had. I am strong and courageous, and I will find someone to love by then!"

Katherine made a promise to herself that life from here on out would include a new love—no matter what.

Katherine was fulfilling her promise to herself and she had been talking to two men over the last two and a half weeks, and was currently in the process of narrowing it down to the one she would meet first and date. Since she hadn't dated in years, she felt that she would pick one guy and date him, rather than dating both guys and then making a choice. She just wanted him to be an average man, a down-to-earth or go-with-the-flow type of guy. She wasn't quite ready for anyone with issues.

Joseph was fifty-two years old, six foot three inches, slightly buff, owned his own auto repair business and enjoyed his hobby, a motorcycle. Christopher was six foot, fifty-four years old and was a truck driver, who was often on the road in various states. She liked them both and they each had several things in common, but Joseph seemed to be a more exciting person to date.

So, Katherine finally decided on Joseph, since he said that he was just an "average Joe," and they both liked dining out and horror movies. Plus, she felt good that he owned his own business. After all, she wanted to find happiness in another satisfying and fulfilling average relationship, and hoped that this might be it.

Katherine was excited about her choice and she would try to keep a positive attitude about the whole dating situation. She was very enthusiastic about possibly going from love lost to love found. She truly believed that this new journey would be a turning point in her life. With that last thought, the phone rang.

She looked at the caller ID and said, "Hello, Joseph.

How are you doing today?"

"Fine. Maybe a little tired, because I just got off work. And you?"

"I'm great!"

"That's a good sign. I'm rather excited that we will finally see each other on Saturday evening. How about you?" Joseph said.

"Me, too. I feel sort of like a teenager going out on a first date. It's been such a long time."

"I know what you mean. This is my first attempt at dating too, since my wife died three years ago."

"Yeah, and that's why I decided to try a widowhood dating service, so I could be with someone who has been through a similar experience in life."

"Now, tell me what you look like again? I didn't want to exchange photos because I wanted to see you in person for the first time."

"Well, I was never a raving beauty, but I was always confident of my looks when I was younger, and I liked to think I could turn the occasional head then and hopefully now. I'm five foot five inches and I have blonde, shoulder-length hair, and my eyes are green. I only wear my glasses when I have to read something. I wear a size fourteen dress. That's my story and I'm sticking to it. So, hopefully, I won't be too hard on your eyes," Katherine said as she laughed.

"I'm sure you are as beautiful as I have imagined."

"Thanks. Now, refresh my memory on what you look like."

"A little taller than the average guy, I work out at the gym every chance I get, so no beer belly, and I'm getting a few gray hairs around my temples. I hope the gray doesn't scare you away," Joseph declared and gave a hearty laugh, too.

They talked for a little while longer, because Katherine had to get off the phone to run some errands before cooking dinner. She was excited after talking to Joseph and glad to see her love life improving. The anticipation of a date seemed so refreshing. At times, the loneliness and sadness of her husband's death seemed like long ago, and sometimes, it seemed like yesterday. Today, it seemed like long ago. She started singing, "Happy days are here again..."

It seemed like forever, but Saturday finally came. Katherine wanted to look extra special. By the third outfit, she was satisfied that she had found the perfect one. She chose a green sundress, which matched her emerald green eyes, and she topped it off with a short sleeve, white jacket. Admiring herself in the mirror, she was so glad that she had splurged yesterday on a younger-looking hairstyle and had convinced herself to add a manicure and pedicure, as well.

She thought, *If this is going to be my second time around on the dating scene, then I'm going to do it in style!*

Katherine gave her reflection a big, approving smile and she was ready for her date.

They had agreed to meet in the parking lot of Carrabba's Italian Grill™. They both liked Italian food. Joseph had a bouquet of flowers for Katherine and kissed her gently on the cheek.

"Katherine, you look so lovely! I feel privileged to be on a date with you," Joseph informed her.

"Thank you, Joseph. I am so happy to finally meet you in person," Katherine added.

"Please, call me Joe. All of my friends do,"

"Thanks, Joe. I will. And my friends all call me Kathy."

"Great. We are off to a good start," Joseph said. And they both chuckled.

The waitress seated them in a cozy corner. They had a delicious dinner and shared some great conversation. Then, two hours later, they emerged from the restaurant—both happy... and smiling from ear-to-ear.

Chapter Two

"Today is my birthday! Imagine a half-century of life. I have restored my confidence and optimism. I feel as though I can leave cares and worries behind me. I can embrace life," she marveled to herself.

She got out of bed and walked over to the mirror. She said, "Katherine, I love you, and girl, age is just a number."

Her cell phone rang. "Hello, Joe."

"Hi, Kathy. Happy Birthday to you. Happy Birthday to you. And may you have many more," Joe sang with a good tone.

"Thanks so much."

"Are you ready for this evening? I have something very special planned for us," Joe said with a smile in his voice.

"Yes, sweetheart. I'm ready!"

"Well, Kathy, put on your best dress and some comfortable dancing shoes, because we are going to paint the town red!" Joe bragged.

"I will be ready with bells on."

"I'll see you at 7:00. Bye, baby."

"Bye."

Katherine got off the phone and realized that her life had made a one hundred and eighty degree turn in just a few short weeks. She was elated.

Joe kept his promise. They painted the town royal red. They had a delicious dinner with all the trimmings, and a small birthday cake for dessert at a local steak house. Then they went to the Rooftop Nightclub. The club was super nice inside, and they played some pretty cool music all night. The place was packed and the music was loud, but it was a pleasant change of pace for both of them.

A local TV celebrity was having his fiftieth birthday party also, and invited Joe and Kathy to join them. When they sang "Happy Birthday," the celebrity invited Kathy on stage with him and they were showered with confetti.

Joe and Kathy laughed, danced, and enjoyed themselves until the wee hours of the morning.

Katherine hadn't enjoyed herself this much in years. Her birthday was a complete success, and she thanked God for the changes in her life—especially for her new love, Joe.

As each day passed, Kathy and Joe seemed to be more and more compatible.

Six Months Later

Katherine's cell rang and Joe's picture popped up. He started talking before she could get a word in.

"Hey, Kathy. It's our six-month dating anniversary. I have something special planned for you at my place. Do you want to come over, or do you want me to pick you up?"

"No problem. I can drive over."

"Okay. How about around sevenish?"

"Yes, I'll be there with bells on."

"Goodbye, baby. I'll see you when you get here."

"Bye."

Katherine wondered what the surprise would be, but decided that it was just a special dinner that he had prepared. She seemed to be on edge all day—jittery—like a teenager.

The hour had finally arrived and it was time for her bath and personal ritual for a date with Joe. She put on a nice beige and brown pants suit and some flats and her leather coat. One last look of approval in the mirror and she was ready to go to his place.

Katherine arrived promptly, and she could tell that Joe had spent a lot of time on this evening. Joe's dining room table was decorated nicely with flowers and candles as a centerpiece. He had the table set with real china and a silver flatware set. Joe had prepared steaks, baked potatoes, asparagus, and dinner rolls, with a chilled bottle of Cabernet Sauvignon.

"Have a seat, Kathy, while I get the food."

"Wow! Everything looks so nice, Joe."

"Yeah, for my special lady!"

"Aw, Joe, you a make a girl blush."

"And I have your favorite dessert, too—cheesecake."

"You remembered."

"Of course, I did."

With that, Joe brought out the food. And they enjoyed a delicious meal and dessert.

"Now, let's go into the family room to sit and relax."

Katherine had never been in Joe's family room before. It was more like a man cave than a family room. A giant big screen TV over the fireplace, auto repair books stacked in the corner, and a small table covered with a confederate flag. There was a picture of his wife on the mantle.

She was looking at the picture when Joe walked in with two glasses of wine.

"Have a seat on the couch. I want to discuss something with you, and then we will have a toast to us and six months of dating."

"Sounds great to me."

Joe set two glasses of wine on the coffee table and he got down on bended knee.

Katherine covered her mouth with her hand.

Joe said, "I love you with all my heart. Although, we've only been with each other for a few months, my love for you grows with each day. You are a beautiful and caring person, and I would like to spend the rest of my life with you. We both have lost our previous spouses, and we will never find a mate exactly like our first. My sons adore you, and I cannot imagine my life without you in it. Now, we have a lot of things to work out, like where to live and merging our lives together, but you can make me the happiest man alive, if you say yes."

Katherine had tears in her eyes and could hardly speak. She mumbled, "Yes"

Joe said, "I didn't hear you."

"Yes. Yes," Katherine chorused.

Joe kissed Katherine on the lips and said, "Now, a toast to us and planning our marriage, and buying you a ring tomorrow."

Chapter Three

Kathy and Joe continued to enjoy themselves and went to dinner every Saturday, often trying a different restaurant. It was always a special time for them to share the week's activities. This week, Joe drove a few extra miles, so they could eat at John Elway, the former NFL player's restaurant. They had heard about his specialties. Joe ordered the buffalo ribeye and Kathy ordered the salmon topped with shrimp and lumped crab. Joe had suggested that they get different orders, so they could try both. The meals were delicious.

However, half way through dinner, a kid at the table across from them was screaming his head off. Joe immediately became upset.

"Look at that couple. They obviously don't know how to raise a kid."

"They look like a regular couple to me," Kathy commented.

"He's white and she's black, and it looks like they have a half-breed on their hands."

Kathy thought, *Obviously, Joe didn't mean that like it sounded.*

"Yeah, some young people don't discipline their kids now days. They both work and leave raising the kids to their nanny or grandma," Kathy added.

"Look at that kid. Now, he's jumping up and down like he doesn't have any sense. And the mother is screaming at the kid. That is so annoying, especially in public!" Joe was obviously perturbed.

"Joe, don't get yourself all worked up over a kid. Sweetheart, just enjoy your meal and ignore them."

Joe started eating again, but seemed overly frustrated. Kathy and Joe were quiet for what seemed like a long time.

"See, they're leaving," Kathy informed Joe.

"Good, because I couldn't stand it much longer, and I was about to ask them to leave anyway. Good riddance!"

Joe finally calmed down once the unruly family left. Once again, Kathy and Joe enjoyed their meal.

Three Months Later

Katherine was excited because her best friend, Mary, was coming to visit for a week to help her make plans for the wedding. The wedding date had been set—the one-year anniversary of when they met. Kathy and Mary hadn't seen each other in a couple of years, but when they did, it was always like they had seen each other yesterday.

Joseph and Katherine were both ecstatic and could hardly wait on their new beginning. Like most men, Joe left planning the wedding to Kathy and her friend.

He had told her on more than one occasion, "You make the plans and just tell me where to be and what to wear, and I'll be there on time."

No matter how much time had passed since high school, whenever Kathy and Mary saw each other, they couldn't resist reminiscing about high school. They were both cheerleaders and they always dug out the old yearbook. So, the night before Mary was to arrive, Katherine asked Joe to come over after work to help find her yearbook in the garage.

They were going through the old boxes and he found a wedding picture of Katherine and her husband.

He stared at the picture for a long time and his face turned beet red.

Joe said, "This is your husband, Billy… that you were married to for twenty-six years?"

"Yes, I have told you all about him."

"Yes, you told me everything about him, except the most important thing—he's black!"

"I didn't think it mattered."

"I hate niggers. I would never hire one in my shop because of the RQ chart!"

"What is the RQ chart? I have never heard of it."

"The Race-Ability Quotient. You know, blacks aren't as intelligent as us whites!"

"I hate them. I believe in white supremacy!"

"You were married to one of them for twenty-six years. No. No. I can't marry you."

Joseph dropped the wedding picture and Katherine could hear the glass and her life shattering. Joseph left immediately.

Joe wouldn't answer Kathy's calls to his house or his cell phone.

Katherine decided that Joseph would come to his senses by the next morning.

She just couldn't figure out how she missed the signs. Then it dawned on her—two blaring red flags. The first indication—his outburst at the restaurant—was about the integrated couple's kid making a scene. She realized that it wasn't at all about the kid's behavior; it was about a white man with a black wife—what did he call their kid? A half-breed.

The silent indication—a confederate flag on his table in the family room.

She relived every moment they had spent together to try to figure out how she missed the signs. She cried herself to sleep.

She stopped by his house on the way to the airport to pick up Mary. Joe's truck was there, but he wouldn't answer the door. She knocked so long and hard that her knuckles were sore, and she was sure the neighbors could hear her knocking.

Why wouldn't Joe talk to her?

Mary knew something was wrong, the moment she saw Kathy. When they got in the car, Kathy broke down in tears, and her whole body started to shake.

Between the tears and the shaking, Kathy told Mary the whole story—every sordid detail.

"Mary, I don't understand. He always treated me with respect, kindness, and love. I had no idea that he was a racist."

"That's because you're white. Racists very rarely let other whites—except their buddies—know how they really feel. It is a hatred imbedded in them stemming from some personal issue."

"All last night, I thought about every conversation we've ever had, and I remembered three times. Once, when we were in a restaurant, he ranted over this integrated couple's kid's behavior and called him a half-breed. During Black History Month, he gave me a spiel on why we should have White History Month. Then month's later, when I went in his family room, I saw a confederate flag displayed on a table."

"Obviously, he has some complicated issues around race. Somewhere, I read that there is a thin line between the behaviors of a racist and a white supremacist. The confederate flag is a symbol of an angry racist and a symbol of hatred. Besides that most racists do not recognize that they are racists."

The friends were quiet for a moment, as if they were both thinking about the meaning of the whole situation.

Then Mary speculated, "Kathy, it's probably better that you found out now, before you got married."

"Yes, you're right, but it hurts to have thought that I had found the man of my dreams and my second husband. He understood widowhood, so well. I should have known it wouldn't be that easy to find another relationship. When it seems too good to be true, it usually is."

"But you have to look at the bigger picture—that hatred was deep inside of him, especially if it will stop him from marrying a woman that he loves, who isn't even black."

"Well, as an educated white person, I repudiate racism because it springs from ignorance! It will take time for me to get over this, but I just have to move on!"

THE END

Rape's Revenge

Chapter One

"I will kill him when I see him," Brenda screamed when the police identified her boyfriend as the suspect who had raped her thirteen-year-old daughter.

"Ma'am, I didn't hear you say that. Now, statutory rape is considered rape and abuse of a child, and if he gets convicted, then he may be punished by a life sentence in state prison," the officer advised Brenda.

Denise had confided in the officer that the attacker was her mom's boyfriend. Denise didn't want to betray anyone or make her mother mad, but the policewoman had convinced her to tell her who did this horrible thing to her.

Brenda's the forty-one-year-old mother of three girls—Denise, thirteen; Deidre, ten; and Deborah, seven. She had been dating Jack, thirty-two, for two years. After such a devastating divorce, she was delighted to finally be dating—much less, a younger man. She trusted him to be around her children, but she had no idea he would harm one of her girls. Brenda pulled herself together with what little dignity she had left, and went to the hospital to pick up her baby.

Brenda walked into the Emergency Room where Denise was sitting on the gurney. Her daughter looked confused and frightened. It was up to Brenda to give her comfort and support.

She immediately hugged and kissed her child and said, "Denise, I love you. He is an adult and he should have known better, but some adults are just plain stupid."

Denise didn't say anything; she just cried and laid her head on her mother's shoulder. When the nurse was finished with her medical care, Denise got dressed, while the nurse told Brenda about the signs of rape trauma syndrome. As the nurse was talking to Brenda, tears streamed down her face, but she didn't utter a sound. She wiped the tears away, before she turned around, because she was determined to be strong for her little girl. Brenda hugged her baby again, and they went home to begin to heal.

The medicine the doctor gave Denise made her sleepy. Brenda was hopeful that now her baby could rest. She went to her bedroom and closed the door, so she could talk privately on the phone. She called her mother.

"Mom," she mumbled and started crying again.

"Sweetheart, I know what happened. Your sister called and filled me in on the details. Have you had a chance to pray, yet?"

"Yeah, I prayed that God will kill him before I get a chance to kill him!"

"Brenda, don't talk like that. You know the Bible says

that 'Vengeance is mine sayeth the Lord.' You need to put the whole situation in God's hands."

"In God's hands... why did He let this happen to my baby? Why?"

"Brenda, you know that God never gives you more than you can bear."

"Mom, get a grip. This is more than I can bear. Jack raped my thirteen-year-old baby. I will kill his damn ass, as soon as he gets out of jail."

"Now, it's your turn to get a grip! What good will it do for you to kill Jack? Yes. He will be dead and you will have revenge, but what will happen to your girls? You will be in prison. Their dad doesn't want them. I am too sickly to properly take care of them. And your sister has three kids of her own. Do you want them in the welfare system? Think about this... seriously."

"Mom, he needs to hurt permanently for all of the hurt and pain that he has caused Denise... and me."

"That may be true, but Romans 12:19 reads 'Beloved, never avenge yourselves, but leave it to the wrath of God, for it is written, Vengeance is mine, I will repay, says the Lord.' Brenda, you must let God handle this for you."

"If God had been in the picture in the first place, He wouldn't have let this happen!"

"Brenda, watch your mouth. Maybe you need another scripture. How about Deuteronomy 32:35, which reads, 'Vengeance is Mine, and retribution, In due time their foot will slip: For the day of their calamity is near, and the impending things are hastening upon them.' Brenda, I raised you to believe in God and read His Word. Have you forgotten your upbringing?"

"No, Mom. But this is different. This is the real life of a child we are talking about—a child, who was violated by a dumb ass man—a man who was seeking power over an innocent child. I am going to get revenge. I am going to kill him."

"Sweetheart, I am going to pray for you. But I want you to get on your knees when you get off this phone and ask God to guide you. Put the whole situation in His hands and let Him deal with Jack. I love you. Please, Brenda!"

"Okay, Mom. I will pray on it. I love you, too. Goodbye."

"Bye, and remember to pray."

Brenda hung up the phone and thought, *I am going to pray all right—that I get his ass before God does!*

Then Brenda went to check on Denise.

That night was a very difficult night for Brenda and Denise. Denise woke up several times after having nightmares. Brenda consoled her child and tried to sleep, but sleep eluded her. All she could think about was ways to kill Jack. She wanted to torture his dumb ass. She wanted him to suffer... immensely. So, she decided to set him on fire.

Chapter Two

Jack had been in jail almost two weeks, while his family was trying to gather bail money. Brenda had thought of a million ways to get revenge.

Somehow, she always felt solitude sitting in her car and thinking things out. Brenda thought, *I'm sitting in my car, thinking… just thinking. I'm angry. I'm hurt. I feel betrayed and I want rape's revenge. I want to kill him. I know there's a big change headed in my direction and I'm not sure what it is. I keep thinking of my three girls that are depending on me. Whatever I decide to do for revenge, it has to work for all four of us. I have to make it work, there's no other option. Failure is not an option. My faith is weak and getting weaker by the moment. Even so, God keeps reminding me that I've been in an indecisive place before. I made it then, and I survived. And I will do it again. It just takes time. I know God is good. I just have to think this over… really good. I am sure that God will help me get through this situation, even though I'm angry with Him. I am just so angry that it happened. God, why would you let this happen to my baby? She's just a child. The bible says, 'God will never give you more than you can bear.' I just don't think I can bear this! God, help me. Please, God, help me.*

With tears streaming down her face, Brenda drove home. All the way driving home, she was blinded by her thoughts and her tears. Yet, she wanted to be in familiar surroundings, so that she could think clearer and she could hear what God had to tell her.

The next morning, a call woke Brenda up. A policewoman at the precinct gave her a head's up. Jack's family had finally gotten enough money together for his bail, and he would be released in a couple of hours.

Brenda was upset. She knew what she had to do.

She had decided to catch Jack off guard at his apartment before he had a chance to hide somewhere. After having run this plan over and over and over again in her mind, she was ready to put it into action.

Being her mother's child, she prayed a quick prayer. She exclaimed, "God, I pray for Your will to be done. Amen."

Brenda dropped her girls off at her sister's place and headed straight to Jack's apartment. She had gone over the way she was going to kill him hundreds of times. Jack's apartment had one way in and one way out. She would douse him with a five-gallon bucket of gasoline and set him on fire with a butane lighter, one with a long arm's length, so she wouldn't get burned. Then she would set the entrance on fire. He would have to jump out of a window and he lived on the fifth floor, or he would have to try to get through the burning exit. So, either way, he would probably die.

It was all in slow motion for Brenda…

She banged on Jack's door.

Jack opened the door.

She threw the gasoline on him and covered his body.

She had the butane lighter ready to ignite the gas and watch the flames cover his body.

Just at that vital moment… God spoke to Brenda, "Revenge is mine." And she couldn't push the button to set Jack on fire.

Jack was screaming, "You crazy bitch, stop it!"

Brenda hissed, "Yeah, I'm a crazy bitch, the one who will kill your dumb ass!"

Jack slammed the door, and Brenda calmly walked to her car.

Brenda didn't go home. She didn't call her mother. She didn't pick up her girls. She had to think… *She had to figure out why she didn't push the button and burn his ass. Why wasn't he currently charcoal? Why was he still alive? And… why she*

*didn't get **her** revenge?*

Brenda finally went home and called her mother.

"Mom, I couldn't do it. I froze. I doused him with gasoline, but I couldn't light the fire."

"Thank God, Brenda! I prayed that God would intervene before you did something that you would regret for the rest of your life."

"I kept seeing my girls crying and screaming, 'Where is my mommy?'"

"I wanted to do it, but I just couldn't."

"Thank you, Jesus."

"Mom, I gotta go."

Brenda hung up the phone and laid down to rest.

The phone rang and it was her sister. She told her that Jack had decided not to press charges against her for the assault and he was going into hiding.

Brenda woke up and drove to Jack's apartment again. His convertible was still parked in his parking spot. It was his prized possession. He loved that car more than he loved anything. He washed it and shined it down, every day. Brenda took her keys out of her purse and keyed it— on all four sides. She smiled as she drove away.

Then the smile disappeared and she drove back to his apartment. She didn't have a knife in the car, so she got the screwdriver out of the trunk. She punched holes in his ragtop and ripped it over and over and over again... like Jack had ripped her heart open.

She thought, *This is my revenge for now.*

Chapter Three

Six Months Later

Denise was showing tremendous progress with her counselor. Because of the statutory rape status, Brenda's insurance had provided a private counselor for one hour a week with a maximum of fifty-two weeks. She was thankful for this. Denise finally believed that she had the right to tell and she was reassured over and over that it was not her fault. Denise was responding well to the sessions with her counselor and to the bi-weekly group sessions with other abused children. Her nightmares had subsided. Brenda was so surprised that Denise was doing better in so little time, and her therapy had helped a great deal, but her life would still be scarred.

Brenda was providing the support that Denise needed. She went to counseling with Denise. She also went to the caregiver's sessions to discuss her anger towards the rapist without Denise hearing her thoughts. Deep down inside, Brenda felt the pain of having brought Jack into her children's lives and she somehow felt responsible for all of the suffering, including her own.

One day after one of the counseling sessions, Denise had confided in Brenda that she was afraid to open up and talk to her about the incident for fear of being misunderstood. Denise confessed that she thought she could handle it alone. But the counselor had convinced Denise that she could trust her mother and that they should talk it over.

Denise said, "Mom, she said that if I talk, then you would listen. Is that true?"

"Yes, Denise. I will listen to whatever you have to say and I will not judge."

Brenda and Denise hugged, cried and talked. This opened a new bonding for mother and daughter.

Life was finally getting somewhat back to normal. Brenda had even agreed to go to church with her mother on a trial basis. Her mother had insisted that she repair her broken status with God.

Brenda had begun to move on with her life and hadn't tried another attempt on Jack's life. But… Brenda continued to silently pray for the vengeance of God on Jack. She didn't quite understand why Jack's trial was taking so long; other than to let Denise have a chance to heal.

One of Brenda's co-workers, Terrance, had tried to reach out to her during this stressful time. He had taken her to dinner on two or three occasions to try to show her that all men weren't perverts. He treated her like a princess, and she was thankful for his concern. One evening, after a great dinner at a nice restaurant, they had a heart-to-heart conversation.

"Brenda, I think you should get back into the dating game. I would love to date you. You are such a nice person to spend time with."

"Terrance, I appreciate the offer; however, I think it will be a long time before I can trust another man around me, let alone around my kids."

"Well, I don't think it's fair to me or you. But I will always be here for you, and I am willing to wait until you're ready to date again."

"Thanks, Terrance. No offense, but I think my girls will be grown and out of harm's way before that will happen. I just don't trust men."

"In the interim, we can still go out to dinner and talk on occasion."

"Okay, but I can't promise that things will change any time soon."

"Like I said before, I'm willing to wait. Just let me know when you are ready."

Brenda gave Terrance a friendly hug and they got in their cars and each went their separate way.

On the drive home, Brenda gave some thought to what Terrance had said and decided to call her sister when she got home after she picked up the girls from her mom's.

She waited until the girls were tucked in and she was ready for bed. In the privacy of her room, she called her sister.

"Hey, Sis, I want to run something by you."

"Go ahead. I'm here for you."

"I went to dinner with Terrance again."

"How was it? Is he still the perfect gentleman?"

"Yes, as always. But he wants to date me. What do you think I should do?"

"Are you ready to date again?"

"No. Not really. But I do miss the companionship of a partner."

"Then wait until you're ready. Wait until your woman's intuition feels right about it."

"Yeah. You're right."

"Can I ask you something that's been bothering me?"

"Sure, go ahead."

"Why do you think Jack did it?"

"Because he's stupid."

"No, seriously."

"Well, he got married when he was sixteen to his first wife, and she was fifteen. I can only speculate. I don't know why he did it. You know, I thought about it, too. I felt betrayed by Jack and I was very disappointed with his behavior. He let me down tremendously. But I've been praying and asking God to take care of the matter."

"Speaking of God, mom told me that you and the girls are going to church with her on Sunday. She's excited every time that you agree to go."

"Yes, she keeps reminding me that I was brought up in the church and that I need to start coming back on a regular basis."

"That's mom, alright."

Both sisters laughed. Then it was quiet for a long moment.

Brenda's sister said, "Are you still paranoid about letting Denise out of your sight?"

"I'm still a little scared, but I'm getting better with each passing day."

"That's great! Brenda, I keep all of you in my prayers daily."

"Thanks, Sis. I need it. We all need it. Well, I've had a big evening and I need to get some rest. I will talk to you tomorrow. Goodnight."

"Goodnight. Love you."

"Love you, too."

Chapter Four

It had been almost a year since it happened. The public defender was swamped with cases, and Jack's case had been postponed more than once. Jack was still out on bail and his trial was scheduled in a few weeks. Brenda was beginning to get nervous about what she would do if the jury acquitted him.

She silently prayed. Then, she thought, *I'll let go and let God.*

Then, a week before the trial, Brenda saw Jack driving down the boulevard with his top down like he didn't have a care in the world. She chased him for several blocks and finally decided it was just not worth it.

She pulled over to think.

Jack continued driving fast and swerving in and out of traffic like a maniac. He looked back at Brenda and laughed. He didn't notice the eighteen-wheeler and the red light.

Jack was killed instantly!

Brenda murmured, "Vengeance is truly Yours, God."

THE END

A Sisterhood of Women Living Life:

Dark Secrets and White Lies

Dark Secrets and White Lies

Chapter One

"Hey, this is call worthy," said Maria to her best friend Nikki.

"Okay. I have some time. Go ahead," Nikki replied.

"Well, you know I'm dating Tommy and Dayvon. I love them both, but I cannot decide who I love the most."

"Hmmm."

"I have a problem—I'm pregnant."

"Hmmm."

"Are you listening to me?" Maria asked with agitation.

"Yes!"

"Well, there's more. Today, I had an ultrasound, and I'm pregnant with twins."

"Oh, I am so sorry."

"You don't sound very supportive for my BFF."

"I am. I'm here for you. But I warned you about dating two guys and having unprotected sex with both of them. I don't want to say I told you so, but as my grandma always tells me, 'you made your bed and now you have to lie in it.' Have you told the guys yet?"

"No. I wanted to talk to you first."

"Well, I think you should tell them—both—as soon as possible."

"Yeah, you're right. Okay. But I have to think about what I want to say—to each of them. Talk to you later."

"Okay, Bye."

Maria got off the phone with Nikki. She had been her best friend since junior high—almost fifteen years—and they shared everything—even clothes, sometimes. Maria knew that Nikki would be the first person that would find out about her pregnancy. They always told each other their darkest secrets. Lately, Maria had a lot of secrets.

Maria started assessing her life—she was twenty-four-years old, and had been with her company since high school. She was dating two wonderful guys, and just wanted to be carefree and happy. She had read an article in a magazine that said women who date multiple men at once must be a cheater, a commitment-phobe, or at a minimum, a liar. Maria didn't think she fell into any of those categories. She just wanted to use her power of choice. Her only regret was that she didn't know who was the father of her babies.

Finally, after all of the thinking, she came to the conclusion that this was a hell of a bad time to be pregnant—no matter who was the father. She was starting a new training program at work that would take four to eight months. She would need full concentration on the job and there was absolutely no time for morning sickness.

She thought, *I wonder whose baby this is—Tommy's or Dayvon's.*

But this was the least of her worries. How could she have had sex with two totally different men? She thought about them both—and who might be the possible father of her babies. Tommy is six foot three inches, slim build, with blond hair and sky blue eyes. He is kind, caring, serious, and so lovable. He has a stable job as a Fed-Ex delivery driver. While Dayvon is six foot four inches, medium build, with black hair and velvet brown eyes. He is playful, joking, funny, and sometimes gullible. He has a job as a manager at the local McDonald's. The guys were almost the same; yet, so opposite. Tommy was white and Dayvon was black.

She knew that her babies would be multi-racial no matter who the father was, because of her Hispanic heritage.

The last few years had been hard for Maria, as she had tried to navigate her life between the American culture and the Hispanic culture. Regardless of her culture, her life choices after high school—for better or worse—had quickly transitioned her from a teen to an adult. Now, she was pregnant and about to be a mother of two. She was raised as a Catholic, although, she had only been to mass a few times since high school, her upbringing definitely ruled out an abortion.

Maria sat on her bed for hours thinking about her life and trying to figure out what was the best thing to do for her and her babies, and what to say to Tommy and Dayvon. She finally decided that she would tell each that she was pregnant with twins. But she wouldn't tell either that there was another man who could possibly be the father. That would be her little dark secret.

Chapter Two

Well, this is it—the day I tell my baby's daddy that I'm pregnant—with twins.

Discussion with Tommy

"Tommy, you know I love you very much, and I have to tell you something that is very important," Maria fretted.

"Let me guess, you got a promotion and we have to move to Alaska?" Tommy jokingly said.

"Quit playing around. This is serious."

"Okay, I'm sorry, go ahead. I'm ready for the good news."

"I'm pregnant."

"Really? Wow! What a blessing. We're going to have a bundle of joy. So, when are you going to marry me?"

"Tommy, will you still want to get married, if I tell you that I'm having… twins?"

"A double blessing. Two bundles of joy!"

"I thought you'd be upset."

"I love you, and I want to spend the rest of my life with you. Let's celebrate."

"I love you, too. But, I have to go to work now. Maybe, we can celebrate later."

They kissed each other goodbye.

Wow. That went better than I thought it would.

Discussion with Dayvon

"Dayvon, I love you very much, and I have to tell you something that is very important," Maria fretted a second time.

"I'm all ears… what's up?" Dayvon chortled.

"I'm pregnant."

"Are you serious?"

"Yes, Dayvon, I'm very serious. But there's more. I'm pregnant with twins."

"Do twins run in your family?"

"No, do they run in yours?"

"No."

"Hey, man, I got super sperm. Two babies in one shot."

"I thought you would be upset."

"I love you and we have a lot going on for us. Do you want to get a two-bedroom apartment together before the twins get here?"

"Let me think about that for a minute and I'll get back to you. But, now, I have to go to work. How about a kiss?"

"You got it!"

Dayvon gave Maria a passionate kiss. After all, she was going to be the mother of his twins.

Wow. That went better than I thought it would. Well, I didn't mention that there is a possibility of a second father to Tommy or Dayvon, but for now that is my secret. I need to discuss this with Nikki.

Discussion with Nikki

"Hey, this is call worthy, again," said Maria to her BFF Nikki.

"Okay."

"Well, I told them both that I'm pregnant with twins, and they both are excited."

"But did you tell them about the other one?"

"No, that's my little secret for right now. I will tell them later."

"Later? I think they should know up front—before you have the twins. Why are you waiting?"

"I'm waiting on the 'right' time to tell them."

"The right time should have been before you got pregnant."

"Maybe you are right, but that's not how it turned out."

"You aren't being honest with them and they have a right to know. Each is the possible father."

"Nikki, you are too much into doing the right thing. Is it because you're a paralegal?"

"No, it's because I have a conscious. And you need to get one—fast."

"Yeah, yeah. I will soon. I gotta get ready for work. Talk to you later."

"Bye, Maria."

Wow. That didn't go well at all.

Maria was doing a pretty good job at keeping the fathers apart, even though her secret kept her juggling situations on a daily basis. Nikki kept reminding her to tell them about the situation, which caused Maria much frustration and agony.

Both guys wanted to go with her to her doctor's appointments, but she insisted on going alone. However, she regretted the decision on her twenty-fifth week check-up.

Maria went to the doctor by herself for this routine check-up. She was at the doctor's office for a very long time, and she was beginning to get nervous, then the nurse finally told her that the doctor wanted to admit her to the hospital for an overnight observation, because she was having Braxton Hicks contractions. This turn of events made her even more nervous.

Maria became alarmed and told the nurse, "But I didn't feel anything different."

"Yes, but when the doctor gave the examination, you were having contractions for fifteen to thirty seconds, which caused your abdomen to become very hard and strangely contorted. So, he wants to observe you in the hospital overnight. It is purely a precaution." The nurse smiled, as if this was a daily conversation with patients.

The exam room was a little chilly and Maria had shivered three or four times. She had missed lunch and her stomach had started to growl. She had gotten a little more nervous while waiting on the doctor to return.

The doctor finally came into the exam room and told Maria that she was experiencing pre-term labor. Maria was worried because she knew that the babies were less than two pounds each, and the doctor had previously told her that he wanted the twins to be as close to five pounds as possible for their birth.

He explained, "I want to keep you in the hospital overnight, but no more than a couple of days for rest and observation." Then he gave her medication to stop the contractions.

Maria was scared. She didn't want to call Tommy or Dayvon. So, she called Nikki from the hospital. Her voice trembled as she spoke softly and asked her friend to stop by on the way home from work.

But… Tommy came to the hospital as soon as he found out that Maria had been admitted. His cousin, Linda, was a labor and delivery nurse at Provident General Hospital and she recognized Maria when she came in. So, she notified Tommy of the situation.

Maria called Dayvon, but lied to him and told him that her condition was very delicate and she could not have any visitors until, she and the babies were stable. This was partially true, because the doctor wanted Maria to carry the babies at least until the thirty-sixth week of the pregnancy to stay out of the danger zone and visitors were limited.

So, after this pregnancy scare, she let both Tommy and Dayvon go on doctor appointments with her—at different times. The doctor wondered why two different men were so concerned with her pregnancy, but he decided not to ask too many questions. Maria told the doctor that

Tommy was the father and Dayvon was a very close and concerned friend—just a little white lie.

Maria was having second thoughts about keeping this predicament a secret from Tommy and Dayvon. Her worrying about what the possible fathers would think was upsetting her. She had cried most of the night before. She had gotten more and more frustrated and needed advice. So she called Nikki.

A Heart-to-Heart with Nikki

"Hey, this is call worthy, again," Maria reflected to Nikki.

"I'm listening," Nikki replied.

"Well, do me a solid. I've got a lot on my chest, and I really need you to listen and offer me some advice."

"Okay, I can do that."

"I've been thinking about the hurt of secrets, the guilt, and the effect on my relationship with Tommy and Dayvon. I was wrong not to tell them that I was… I mean, I am dating two guys. Initially, I didn't know what the hell to do. I guess, I could've had an abortion, but then God would be mad at me, and Father Donovan would have had me to say a million Hail Mary's. But I wanted to do what was best for the babies. Both fathers are so happy and have been there for me, since I told them that I was pregnant. But the guilt is eating away at me. Honestly, I feel so depressed and I know it's my own doing. I don't know what I was thinking at the time, and I wish some days I'd just had an abortion. It would have been easier. But then I would feel worse because I love my babies, and I haven't even met them. All I wanted was to do what was right by them. I didn't want them growing up without a dad like me and my sisters had to."

The memories, loneliness, and pain of her fatherless childhood flooded Maria's mind and she started crying.

Nikki offered, "You know, dark secrets like this come to light, eventually. It is better that you own up now, and tell Tommy and Dayvon about the situation and let them make a decision on what they want to do. They have a basic right to know the truth. Not to mention—the babies. They need to know who their parents are. What a horrible situation to be in. I really feel for you. But only you know what to do about this. I've never been in your position, but I hope you will find the right answer that you feel is best. Perhaps you should pray on it."

"Yes, I know I should. Sometimes, the choices we make at the time are not the right ones, but what is done is done. I know what I've done is stupid. If I tell them, it will break their hearts. I love them both so much. But I need some more time to think this out a little more."

"Well, good luck. If you need to talk again, call anytime."

"I will. Thanks for listening to me and offering good advice."

"You're welcome. Bye, Maria."

I feel so much better now that I've gotten that off my chest. But I still have to make a decision on whether to tell Tommy and Dayvon before the twins are born.

Maria sighed gently, as a tear rolled down her cheek.

I just need a little more time…

Chapter Three

A few calm weeks went by and then all hell broke loose when Maria had a second pre-term labor at twenty-nine weeks!

Tommy had accompanied her to the doctor's office for this visit.

While waiting in the exam room, she called Nikki to let her know what was happening. Nikki rushed to the hospital to be with her friend.

Maria felt calmer with both Tommy and Nikki at her side. After a few hours in the exam room, the contractions had stopped by themselves. But the doctor wanted to talk to Maria and Tommy about the twin's safety.

The doctor admitted, "I don't expect a full-term pregnancy. It very rarely happens with twins. The main goal of a twin pregnancy is to carry them at least thirty-six weeks. So, we want Maria to carry the babies, as long as she can for the health of your twins. I am going to put Maria on complete bed rest for the next six to eight weeks, or until she delivers. I would like for them to be at least five pounds at delivery. My advice is to get family and friends to help Maria, while she's on bed rest. Make sure she stays off her feet. Even though thirty-six weeks is the target, many twins are delivered early. I'm putting her on bed rest, so she doesn't deliver too early. Any questions, so far?"

"Is this normal?" Tommy asked.

"Yes, for a twin pregnancy, and especially, since this is Maria's first pregnancy. The next few weeks of bed rest will be an emotional and stressful time for both of you. Please try to do the best you can."

Tommy, Maria, and Nikki left the hospital and went to Maria's apartment. Tommy wanted to move in to help, but Maria had an excuse for why he couldn't. After he left, Maria called Dayvon to explain what the doctor had told her and Tommy.

Nikki insisted that she fess up to both fathers. Maria said that she still needed just a little more time to keep her secret.

Delivery Day

Dayvon was with Maria at her apartment trying to keep her company, because she was bored out of her mind with nothing to do, but read and watch movies. In the middle of the movie, Maria screamed and it startled Dayvon, who was half asleep. He realized that she had gone into labor and he rushed her to the hospital.

Tommy's cousin called him, again, to tell him that Maria had been admitted and that she was in a birthing room this time.

Maria was having complications and no one else was allowed in the birthing room for a few minutes. Tommy, Dayvon, and another father were in the waiting room—all nervously waiting to be allowed into the room with their significant other.

Tommy and Dayvon were bragging to each other about having twins the first time out—unaware that Maria was the same mother of their twins.

The doctor came out and told Tommy that they were ready for him to come in for the delivery of the babies.

The first baby girl is born without complications, but with caution. The nurse cleaned her up and handed the newborn to her proud father. The doctor delivered the second baby girl and when she popped out, the doctor said, "Oh, my." The doctor handed the baby to the nurse, who also shrieked, "Oh, my!"

Immediately alarmed, Maria leaned over to see what was wrong with the baby. The nurse rushed the baby off to the clean-up area before Tommy or Maria could see her.

The doctor and the nurse both went to the clean-up area with the baby and were speaking very softly. Maria and Tommy could not hear what they were saying.

The doctor came back into the delivery room and announced, "Maria had twin girls, both babies are just over five pounds and they are doing well." The nurse handed the second baby to Maria.

Maria looked at the baby girl and she too said, "Oh, my." At that point, Tommy got up out of the rocking chair, carrying the first twin, and rushed over to Maria to see why everyone kept looking at the second baby and said, "Oh, My."

Tommy looked at the baby with confusion on his face. He handed Maria the first twin and looked at Maria, straight in the eyes and said, "So, I was just one of your sperm donors. I can see that you're dating more than me. And I loved you so much." Tommy paused as if he was thinking very hard and added, "How could you keep a secret like that? I don't ever want to see you or the babies again!"

He stormed out of the room.

When Tommy came out, he was livid. One baby girl was white and one baby girl was black. He couldn't understand how Maria, the woman that he loved so much, could do this to him.

After Tommy left the birthing room, Maria looked at the doctor and said, "How could this happen? How can I have twins and one is white and one is black?"

The doctor cleared his throat and questioned, "Do you have African Americans in your family?"

"No, but Dayvon is black."

"You mean your friend?"

Maria revealed, "Well, he's a little more than a friend. He could be the father of the babies. I'm ashamed to admit it, but I'm not really sure who the father is."

The doctor said, "So, you really don't know who the

father is?"

"Yes, I'm not sure." Maria quietly added with embarrassment ringing in her voice. She said, "Can twins actually have two different fathers?"

The doctor authoritatively added, "Yes, it's possible, but we would have to have a DNA test to make sure. It's a phenomenon known to the medical community as heteropaternal superfecundation. Here is how it can happen: Two male partners have sex with the same female partner. One man's sperm fertilizes one of the woman's eggs, while the other man's sperm fertilizes another one of her eggs. This all has to happen in within hours or days, since sperm are only viable for about five days. And the twins would be fraternal, not identical."

Maria interjected with tears streaming down her cheeks, "Is this rare?"

"The truth is, nobody knows. I mean, we presume this is rare, but we don't know at all. The babies and possible fathers would have to be tested. If this is what happened in your instance, this would be my first case and I've delivered well over one thousand babies, I haven't seen it, but I did read about it in medical school. The time window when eggs can be fertilized is small. Like I said earlier, it's rare, but not impossible. The key here is that a woman has intercourse with two different men in a short period of time while ovulating, and it's possible for both men to impregnate her separately. The dynamics of the sexual playroom can be very complicated. It's like playing with genetic dice. So, that's the explanation, if this is what happened to you."

"Okay," Maria said quietly. "I kinda knew in the back of my mind that something like this would happen, but I was hoping the babies would look like me."

"Well, I guess, we better get the other father in here… ah, I mean the possible father."

Dayvon was still waiting on the doctor to tell him about his twins. He had waited patiently. He didn't really give it too much thought because the same doctor was the doctor for all three men and the mothers. But he had decided to ask the doctor if Maria was having complications, the next time that he saw the doctor.

Just then, the doctor walked into the waiting room to get Dayvon. He said, "You are the proud father of twin girls, and Maria is doing much better now. Come and see your family."

Dayvon had noticed that the doctor had a funny look on his face, as he escorted him to Maria's room.

Dayvon was so happy when Maria handed him the black baby girl with thick black hair and velvet brown eyes. But his expression quickly changed when she handed him the white baby girl with blonde hair and sky blue eyes.

He looked at Maria and said, "This baby doesn't look like me or you. So, obviously you've had sex with someone else. How could you keep a secret like that? I don't ever want to see you or the babies again!"

Maria cried. She knew that she had played a dangerous game.

Maria was devastated. She had no idea that the fathers would react like this.

And Nikki had warned her to tell the truth to both fathers.

Maria realized that her dark secret was no longer a little white lie. The secret was out in the open. It was right before her eyes in black and white. The dark secret had backfired on her... and her baby girls.

THE END

Really Short

Stories

A Sisterhood of Women Living Life:

Really Short Stories

True Love

They met in high school, and frozen in that perfect moment; they thought it to be true love forever. After finishing college, they realized that perhaps it was just infatuation, and nothing more. So, he went his way and made a life for himself—he got married and had kids. She made a wonderful career for herself and realized that love had eluded her.

Years later, the elderly widower and the old maid met once again, only to fall in love—again.

He said, "You are my soul mate, the one I didn't recognize to be ideally suited to be my romantic partner forever."

She said, "There is no perfect person, but there is perfect love."

THE END

A Haunted House

A chill engulfed my body the moment I entered the haunted house. Looking around the room, I felt bathed in darkness, as my thoughts began to drench me in fear. I saw a broken mirror and I looked in it, only to notice no image looking back at me.

I could smell a burning candle, and when I got close to it, the shadow showed footprints on the ceiling. I reached out my hand to blow out the candle, when suddenly a black cat jumped on me and I heard screaming.

I didn't know if the screams were coming from me or someone else, but I ran for the door. My heart was beating faster and faster as I was trying to open the heavy, wooden front door… then someone touched me and said, "Happy Halloween."

THE END

A Guardian Angel

I glanced at the clock, as we were about to walk to the bus stop to pick up my older daughter from school. Just as I was about to walk out the door with the baby in my arms, I heard the loud screeching of brakes.

All of the mothers began running towards the bus stop, and in my heart, I knew that something eerie had happened. I held the baby close to my body and sprinted the short distance.

When I arrived, the bus driver was crying and she was bending over a child—mine! She had black tire tracks on her new red coat, but the bus had missed her by an inch.

My daughter said, "Mommy, this nice, old lady pushed me out of the way so I wouldn't get hurt!"

THE END

The Artist

Jessica thought about how her day had begun on Venice Beach, and now she felt like a mermaid basking in the sun waiting on Prince Charming. It was like a dream come true—she felt on top of the world with her new friend, Roger, hanging onto her every word.

She wanted to spend more time with him, so she could enjoy his company just a little longer. She only wished that she could meet someone famous and rich, but this handsome man would have to do.

So, she invited him to join her in viewing the new art exhibit down the street, and was delighted when he agreed. They viewed all of the paintings and sculptures, and spent two lovely hours discussing colors, textures and the artistic creativity of the one-man show of John R. Mondavie.

But, just as they were leaving, a young lady approached Roger and asked for his autograph.

THE END

The Stranger

Paige sat and reminisced about her life, when she was jolted out of her private space by a tall handsome stranger.

"Excuse me, Miss, but can you give me directions to the L'Ouvre?" he announced.

"Sure, go to Paris and turn left," Paige sneered.

"That is one of my best lines, and you are the only person who got it," the stranger exclaimed.

"So, what's up with you and the French lines," Paige wondered.

"Well, when I see a beautiful woman in deep thought, I want to join her and… and take her to lunch," the stranger stammered.

"It seems like an interesting suggestion, and I'm free," Paige giggled.

THE END

Sneak Preview

of

Book 2

Sneak Preview

A Sisterhood of Women Living Life:

June's Double Rainbow

June's Double Rainbow

Chapter One

The one who loves opens herself up for hurt and pain.
—Anonymous

September 24th at 12:35pm

Life is about to come to a mind-blowing halt for June Renee Johnson.

June had a busy morning of meetings with important clients and was about to go purchase a new computer when her cell phone buzzed. She was driving and had to pull into the parking lot to answer it, because she had forgotten her bluetooth.

"Hi, Sweetie. How's your day at work going?"

"Hello. Ahh… Hi. I was just about to leave you a message. I thought you said you were busy until 1:00 o'clock."

"I was, but I finished with my meetings a little early."

"I have something I want to discuss with you."

"OK, I am about to go into the store and look for a new PC. Can it wait or do you want to tell me quickly?"

"I can tell you right quick. I have been thinking about it for a long time now and I just want to get it off my mind."

"OK, what is it?"

"I am not happy in the relationship and I think we should both just move on!" he said as nonchalantly, as if he were saying there are no clouds in the sky today.

"What do you mean? I know we have been having problems, but I didn't think they were this serious. I think we should talk about this in person… face-to-face at least, since we are engaged."

"There is no need to talk in person. I have made up my mind and I want to end the relationship!"

The last four and a half years suddenly flashed before her eyes. She met this 6'4" tall, handsome man on one of those online dating services. She was almost thirty and he was thirty something. She had lucked out, Greg was a TV news anchorman with weird working hours and intermittent off days. And she was an architect in a very competitive field with long hours and weird off days. But they had one thing in common—they always made time for each other… quality time. Two years ago they had gotten engaged. He gave her a beautiful birth stone ring encircled in diamonds and they had not had time to set a wedding date or get a proper engagement ring.

"But we're engaged… and we should discuss this," June stammered.

"I told you that I have thought about this. The bottom line is that I don't want to get married. YOU want to get married. I have to go back to work. Bye…" He abruptly declared.

Dial tone.

Despite reeling in the pain of rejection and being emotionally flattened by the hopelessness of it all, June was completely stunned!

Chapter Two

June stares out her window, while driving home—not looking at people, or the traffic or the scenery—not really looking at anything, just thinking about the most devastating conversation of her life. Then, she sat almost in a trance in her driveway and could not tell anyone how she got home or when she got home. Tears streamed down her face and she could hardly see. Surely, this had to be a nightmare and she would wake up any moment.

But she didn't wake up and somehow she knew she was not dreaming. So, she mustered up enough strength to get out of her BMW and walk inside her condo and lock the door behind her.

June's mind was racing faster than any winning car in the Indy 500. She was continually replaying situations out in her mind—her thinking machine. She repeatedly thought about situations that went on in their life in the last six months. She was trying to rationally figure out what triggered this loving, kind man of her dreams to say these mean, hurtful and painful words... *I am not happy in the relationship and I think we should both just move on!*

Her boyfriend of four and a half years was floating in a pool of complacency. She thought about what Pastor Rivers had said on Sunday. "...and the complacency of fools shall destroy them."

June's mind began to explore all of the recent arguments—real and made up. She had noticed over the last six months or so.

She thought, *Greg was constantly trying to pick arguments with me.*

Like when she looked in his phone and saw the nude pictures of another woman. The first picture was of boobs, but the second picture was something else and she kept turning the phone around trying to figure out what it was. When she realized what part of the body it was, she was so shocked and hurt that she immediately deleted it. When she approached him about it, he was more concerned with her looking at his phone and a breach of privacy, than the fact that some woman had sent him naked pictures.

Then there was the time a woman from work had called him three times in one day, while they were enjoying a rare moment of quality time together. On her fourth call, June just went berserk!

She remembered shouting, "Unless it is a family emergency, I would appreciate it if you would not answer your cell phone—period!"

His excuse was that he had to answer his phone to keep in contact with work, in case some great news story broke and he had to go back to the television station.

The latest argument was over an old girlfriend, who would text, email and send pictures all day, like he was her man! June remembered him blowing that off saying that she was having problems with her teenage son and needed a man's advice on steering the young man in the "right" direction.

But then June's thoughts turned to the good memories in the beginning of the relationship. The time they went to Hawaii and they spent time in only two places—on the beach or in the bedroom.

She thought, *I can see us now, walking along the beach holding hands, eating brunch or dinner in restaurants on the beachfront, or just sitting on the beach talking and listening to the waves crashing. We always enjoyed making love instead of eating dinner… yum… yum—and then, waking up to start the process all over again—only this time for breakfast.*

She closed her eyes for just a moment to see him smile down at her and she remembered just barely smelling the scent of love making mixed with the ocean fragrance.

Oh, new love can be so wonderful.

Like walking in the rain—the time he had to emcee the show for "Sweet Honey in the Rock." It was fun, but especially, memorable, when they walked down the street in the mist of rain to the parking lot… singing and holding hands.

Greg can be very loving at special moments.

So, where did things go so wrong that he didn't want to be in the relationship anymore? When did he become complacent?

Complacent. What does it mean?

She jumped up and ran to get her iPhone, so she could look up the meaning online to make sure her mind had not deceived her on the meaning of complacent. She must have read it at least a dozen times.

I know, I just read it—over and over—but it's not sinking in. I think it said that it was a feeling of quiet pleasure, while unconcerned with unpleasant realities. Is marriage the unpleasant reality? Is his complacency destroying our relationship… our marriage… our future together?

She started crying… again. It seemed as though that's all she did lately was cry! It was time for June to do something, instead of crying. So, she got mad.

Oh, hell no, Satan is a liar!

"I am a very intelligent woman; yet, I seem so naïve when it comes to men and relationships. I can handle million dollar projects, but I can't handle one man. What is wrong with *Me*?" she yelled through her tears, as if actually talking to someone, when in all reality she was home alone.

She continued talking to no one in particular, "I once read, I don't know where though. Oh, well, whatever. I think it said that if there is not something specific that directs us concerning a decision or outcome we must make or want, we often look for a sign from God."

June immediately fell on her knees and began praying:

Dear Heavenly Father,
Please help me to understand what is happening and most assuredly why this is happening to me? God, let me

hear your voice. Please in Jesus' name give me wisdom! Amen.

June stopped crying and began listening for the Lord's answer. The room was quiet... all she could hear was the clock ticking.

"God, I talk to you every day and all day long. I have heard you before. Why can't I hear you, now?"

Once again June was quiet as a mouse, as she strained to try to hear something... anything from God. And this is what she heard... silence.

The more she thought about their relationship, the more she realized that it was dysfunctional. Maybe, that's what God wanted her to hear.

Once again, she cried. This time, she got so angry that she wanted to kick Greg's ass. She could not shut him out of her thoughts and she could not break free from the pain.

Then, her emotions became overloaded. She could not cope anymore and the next thing she knew, she had shut down—completely.

June went to bed and stayed there for over 24 hours. She couldn't answer the phone or the door. She could not move. She could not eat. She could not cry. June was shocked into an emotional coma.

Chapter Three

Once she felt better, Phyllis was the only person she had discussed her thoughts and feelings with in the last few days. She had decided that it was time for her to make a change. She had made up my mind. Now, she wanted to call Phyllis and let her know of her decision.

"Hi, Phyllis. I have made up my mind. I am going to Paris!"

"Wait a minute, back up, girlfriend. Where did that come from? A few days ago you were crying because lover boy broke up with you on the phone. Personally, I think that was better than him sending you a text. But, hey, who am I to judge?"

"I thought about it and I thought about it. Actually, I've been thinking about it way too much. I have tried so hard to make this relationship work. Greg's a great guy, but not the most romantic, except in his mind. At times he's insensitive and forgets some important things. Sometimes he's too wrapped up in himself and his job to think about me or my friends. And on occasion, he does take me for granted. The sex is good, but what I have to go through to get it is ridiculous. Greg craves 'visual sex' and he wants me to wear all of those exotic costumes and lingerie to get him aroused. That alone is costing me a fortune. Me… I just crave relationship attention—just give me a little quality time and I'm happy. He used to make time for me, but now he is always so busy with his job. Neither of us is getting what we want, so I guess that's why he's not happy with the relationship. What do you think?"

"Well, I, ah…"

June cut Phyllis off with, "Well, that's it. There just isn't much to say about the relationship—Period. I'm trying to push my pain and disappointment aside, I need to just walk away from people who hurt me or make me suffer. And Greg has done just that. I need to be happy and I think Paris can make me happy. Anyway, I am so excited. It's a last minute decision, but let me tell you about the trip to Paris!"

"OK. Go ahead."

"The American Institute of Architects is having their conference in Paris, next week. Paris is such a beautiful city with so much to do and see and with absolutely delicious food to eat. I think, if I go there for a week, I can get Greg out of my mind. What do you think?"

"Yes, I think you can. So, can I be a stowaway in your luggage. LOL"

"Phyllis, you are crazy. But that's why I love you, girl! Let me go, so I can pack. I will call you tomorrow."

"Okay, sistergirl. Bye."

Look out Paris, here I come! Now, where is my passport?

Chapter Four

As June looks out the airplane window, as they are about to land, she says a quick prayer.

Dear God
I am about to land at the Orly Airport in Paris, France. Please let my life take a new direction. And please let me forget Greg and the last 4 ½ years. Give me love in Jesus name. Amen.

The plane landed and June immediately knew that she had better things awaiting her.

It was late on Wednesday evening; it had been a nine hour flight. June and her co-workers took the shuttle to the Mercure Paris Porte de Versailles Vaugirard Hotel and checked-in. Tomorrow was a jet lag/free day and the conference would start on Friday at the Exhibition Center across the street from the hotel. June and her co-workers—Joseph and his wife, Patricia, architects; and Rebecca, the office administrative assistant—had agreed to meet for a light breakfast and see if they could do some sightseeing.

June woke up well-rested and was looking forward to some delicious French food. She was not disappointed at breakfast. She had a chausson aux pommes—a puff pastry crust filled with a chunky apple filling—and tea.

Yum, yum.

The Concierge had suggested to the small group to try the Big Bus Sight-Seeing Tour. It was a hop-on and hop-off bus to explore the sights. And the hotel was already close to the Champs Elysées, Place de Concorde, luxury shops and the Eiffel Tower, and Trocadéro, so they could venture on to see additional cultural attractions, as well as, the cultural richness of the Palais de Chaillot, the Cité de l'Architecture et du Patrimoine and the Musée de la Marine—an architects dream. They all agreed that they were in the best area of Paris and the planning committee had made a wonderful decision on staying at this hotel.

After about four hours of sight-seeing, they were ready for lunch at an outdoor café. The bus driver suggested one within walking distance of the hotel, just before it started raining. He even had des parapluie—that is umbrellas for a price. But they came in handy for the downpour. It was concurred to eat at Angelina's Restaurant, the brochure named it "The Best in Paris," where Coco Chanel had patronized years ago. Most of the group ordered a Paris lunch—an omelet, salad and a variety of pastries to sample, which melted in their mouths. June also ordered the famous hot chocolate, which was to die for. After a substantially satisfying meal, they decided to walk back to the hotel and if it was too long a walk, they would catch a taxi for the rest of the way. When they walked outside, there was a beautiful double rainbow in the sky. June was the only one standing in the middle of the sidewalk starring at the rainbow, the others had moved aside.

A well-dressed, handsome Frenchman stopped and said to June, "Mademoiselle, si vous prendre une photo, il durera plus longstemps."

She turned and said to the stranger, "Je ne parle pas Français. Je suis Américain."

As she looked into his ocean blue eyes, they formed an instant connection.

"Then perhaps, I can take you to lunch and explain to you what a double rainbow symbolizes."

"Sorry, we just had lunch."

The Frenchman determined to win over this lovely American turned and quickly took a picture of the rainbow and added, "So, can I send this picture to your phone or your email?"

"Maybe. Let me think about it."

"Mademoiselle, my name is Guillaume and yours?"

"My name is June, like the month."

With that her friends joined them and suggested that they walk back to the hotel. June and the French gentleman said their goodbyes and walked in opposite directions.

June regretted that she didn't give the handsome Frenchman her number, email or at least tell him where she was staying.

Oh, well, opportunity lost, she thought.

While she was dressing for dinner, the concierge knocked on her door. He handed her a bouquet of flowers and a small picture. She smiled, because she knew exactly who had sent them.

The Concierge said, "The gentleman who dropped these off said that he did not know your last name, but that you were probably the only American guest named June… And you are the only one, Mademoiselle. He also left this envelope."

He handed her an exquisite envelope made of fine linen stationary and she opened it.

It read, "Mademoiselle June, if you are free for dinner this evening, please call me at my mobile phone number 06 78 90 12 34 and I would be delighted to discuss the double rainbow. If not, please feel free to call me any time. Guillaume or William, whichever is your preference. Until we meet again."

June told the Concierge thank you and handed him a tip.

June called Guillaume and told him that the Concierge had arranged for their group to have dinner and a show at the sold out Moulin Rouge this evening and she would have to take a raincheck for perhaps tomorrow. He agreed and said, "Tomorrow, dinner it is, Mademoiselle June." They each hung up. Each one's smile, enveloped in happiness, was bigger than the other one.

June dressed in a simple, but stunning elegant black dress accessorized with jewelry and her long hair was in an updo style. After one last look in the mirror, she was ready to meet her colleagues in the lobby. The Concierge had arranged for a limo to pick them up and return for them after the show. They were all excited and there was plenty of chitter chatter on the limo ride there. After reaching the Moulin Rouge with the world-famous windmill atop, they waited in line for about an hour before they were seated at the best table in the house—center stage. There were five chairs at their table and they figured a single tourist would join them.

They were served their champagne and just before dinner was served Guillaume slipped into the seat next to June. June was indeed surprised.

The waiter started serving the Soiree Toulouse-Lautrec—Breast of Roasted Chicken from the Landes Region, Shellfish Bisque, Fricassee of Seasonal Vegetables, and the Opera pastry, a homemade Bourbon Vanilla Custard for desert. The food was "magnifique!"

In between bites, she managed to ask Guillaume how he got a ticket to the sold-out show. He said that he had his special way of getting what he wanted, when it involved a beautiful woman that he was interested in seeing. June smiled just as the theatre lights switched off, the curtain was raised and the entire troupe appeared on stage in extravagant costumes, which included lots of feathers, rhinestones, and sequins.

The performance was a sight to see and hear with so many colors, bright lights and so much harmonious music. It was a spectacular 2-hour show.

When the show was over Guillaume kissed June on both cheeks, told her that he would pick her up at her hotel promptly at 7:00 tomorrow evening for their rendez-vous, and disappeared as quickly as he had arrived.

June didn't quite know what to think about this mysterious Frenchman. She thought about him every waking moment for the rest of the evening, until she closed her eyes.

Then she dreamed of him… Guillaume.

Chapter Five

It was the opening day of the American Institute of Architects (AIA) and the brochure read, "A provocative lineup of celebrity speakers with an awe-inspiring array of tours, exhibitors, seminars, and must-see architecture. All happening in the legendary 'City of Lights,' known as a global center for art, fashion, gastronomy and culture. Enjoy three days packed with opportunities."

June's first day was loaded with buzz-worthy speakers and workshops, where she learned and even earned continuing education credits, and discovered the latest products and trends. It was a long, but well-accomplished day of events. June walked into her hotel room at 5:30 and the phone was ringing. She answered it, while taking her shoes off.

It was Guillaume and he was checking to make sure they were still on for tonight's rendez-vous. He had a surprise planned for June. She told him that they were still on, but she needed some time to rest before joining him. Someone at the convention told June that Frenchmen were often rather pushy, almost to the point of being annoying. So, she wasn't surprised at his call.

Guillaume picked June up and the surprise was a dinner cruise on the Seine River aboard the Bateau Le Calife. The boat itself was characteristic, while the glass roof-top offered fantastic views and overall, had the perfect romantic ambiance. There were two eating areas for about 30 people, all of the tables were window seats, and it was ideal for a romantic dinner. The boat was a lovely intimate size and the food was excellent. Le Calife was family-owned sophistication and luxury all the way.

Guillaume had made the perfect choice. There were breath-taking views of Paris at night, and it was truly a "city of lights." But the best part of the evening was when they stopped just beneath the Eifel Tower at 10 pm to catch it in all of its glory with the fantastic 'twinkling lights.'

The Eiffel Tower illuminates and flashes lights, while you enjoy the show. It provided a stunning backdrop and a romantic memory of Paris.

When the cruise was over they headed back to the hotel for a quiet conversation in the wine room to talk and get to know each other a little better.

Guillaume broke the ice, "So, June, let me tell you a little about myself and then you can follow me."

"That would be great."

"Well, I am a third-generation Parisian born and bred. I have a Master of Tourism Administration degree from George Washington University in Washington, DC."

"So, that's how you got the ticket to the Moulin Rouge."

"Yes, I called in a favor. And of course, I know the best places for tourist to sight-see. My parent's business administers events for various tourist businesses. I am 35 years old, single and unattached, which annoys my mother to no end. How about you?"

"I am an architect. Most women graduates do not stay long in the occupation or they marry another architect and start a firm. I've been in the business for nine years, now and my goal is to be a celebrity female architect."

"How is that working for you?"

"I'm fine."

"I can see that." They both laughed.

"I mean, it's going well. I have had several successes. And I'm glad to be in Paris to learn even more."

"I never ask a woman her age, I am assuming you are younger than me."

"Yes, I graduated high school at sixteen and by the time I was 21, I had my Master's degree."

"Interesting. A very intelligent American woman."

They both smiled.

"So, what about your love life? A beautiful, intelligent

woman like you must have a man somewhere in the background."

"I did, but he broke it off a few weeks ago. I was dating… engaged to a TV newscaster."

"His loss is my gain. Are you basically over him? Ah… I don't want to be the rebound guy. I am willing to wait. LOL"

"I think so. At first, I was so hurt that I cried constantly, then I fell into an emotional coma. But every time, I thought about what happened on the day he broke up with me, I lived the bad situation over and over again. I did at some point think about the good things that had transpired in the 4 ½ years we had been together. But that is over now, and I don't want to talk about it."

"Okay. Let's talk about the Double Rainbow. I think it was a sign that things are changing in your life. The double rainbow symbolizes a transformation in life. The first rainbow represents the material. The second rainbow represents the spiritual. So, why do we stop to admire its' beauty? It's meant to help us align both our outer world and our inner spirit. So, when you are unsure about life, look at the picture of the double rainbow and remember what I just said."

"Wow. That makes a lot of sense. I hadn't really thought about it that way before."

"Yes. Hey, it is getting late and you have to get up early for your conference. Let's call it a night, but if you need to talk, just call me."

"Okay. Good night, Guillaume."

"Good night, June"

He kissed June on both cheeks and walked her to the elevator. They both hated to see the door close with each on opposite sides of the door.

Chapter Six

The next few days were a whirlwind of business by day and romance by night. June was enjoying her trip to Paris and had forgotten about her life back home.

Then, suddenly the conference had ended and she had one more day in Paris to sight-see… and spend with her new love. Guillaume had hired a 10-passenger bus to take the small group on a trip to see all of the sights that real Parisians knew about. It was a special treat for June and her co-workers. Of course, they enjoyed the Louvre, the Musée d'Orsay, Galeries Nationales du Grand Palais, Arc de Triomphe, Notre Dame de Paris, Sacre-Coeur Basilica de Montmartre and other sights.

Then, they had dinner at Le Sixieme Sens, which only seats about 20 people. The chef welcomes all of the guests, takes the orders, serves the meals and finds time to have a little chat with guests. He does it all to perfection. The food was delicious and the service was excellent. Guillaume out did himself in putting together a day to remember.

Everyone went back to the hotel to pack their luggage for tomorrow's departure. It was a bitter-sweet end to a lovely trip.

Once again, Guillaume was a perfect gentleman with kisses on each cheek and he promised that he would call June after she returned home.

Once June was on the flight back home, she reminisced about the trip and realized that Guillaume was everything she ever wanted… but she wanted more.

How can your soulmate/your romantic partner—the man with an unbreakable bond—be on another continent… so far away?

As promised, he called June when she arrived home from her trip. They sent texts and used skype or tango to connect on a daily basis.

Then, one day, she hadn't heard from him in about twelve hours. She was on the phone crying and talking to Phyllis.

"He didn't call me this morning. He calls every morning. He must have gotten his bill and decided to cut the long-distance relationship off. What should I do?" June said sobbing into the phone.

"Wait until you find out what is going on. June, I read somewhere that it doesn't matter who hurt you or broke you down. What matters is who made you smile again. And he certainly made you smile again."

"Phyllis, you are always the voice of reason. That's why I love you, girl."

Just then, her doorbell rang. She was still holding the phone in her hand when she answered the door.

She screamed, "It's Guillaume." She dropped the phone.

He showered her with kisses and carried June across the threshold to a new future.

Chapter Seven

September 24th, Two Years Later

June and Guillaume had just returned from their Paris home and were back in the U. S., because they had exciting news to tell her parents and they were going to meet them for an early dinner at Ruth's Chris Steak House, her dad's favorite restaurant.

For this special occasion, June had chosen a designer dress and she looked amazing in the stunning white lace dress. Her face had a special peachy glow and her long hair was flowing in the slight breeze. She bared a bit of her shoulders in the subtly sexy dress. Guillaume smiled at the beauty and elegance of his lady, as they entered the restaurant and heads turned in June's direction.

June's parents were there when they arrived. Greetings were exchanged. Her mom was excited and eager to hear the news.

"Dear, I can hardly wait for you to tell us. I hope it's what I think it is." Her mom smiled as she relayed her happiness.

June boasted, "Well, it's probably not what you're thinking."

"Oh, really?" her dad replied.

"I will let Guillaume tell you. He's so delighted and glad to tell anyone the good news."

"Drum roll… as you know, we've been married for a year and a half now. And…"

"Oh, please, just tell us," her mom begged.

"Okay. Okay. We're pregnant."

"That's wonderful. I'm finally going to be a grandmother!"

"That's not all… we're pregnant with twins."

"Oh, my, I will have two grandkids to play with," her dad opined.

"That's not all… it's a boy and a girl!"

Everyone was so excited about the news that they

almost forgot about eating dinner.

The waiter chimed in, "Are you ready to order or do you need a little more time?"

They all laughed and began looking at the menus. They finally ordered dinner. The excitement and conversations rambled on with joy and happiness.

After an enjoyable meal, the couples left the restaurant. As they were leaving the restaurant, a man passed them in a wheelchair.

He said, "June, is that you?"

June turned around, because she didn't recognize the older man.

She said, "Sir, do I know you?"

"Yes, it's me, Greg. I know that I look different, because I was recently in a car accident."

"Oh, I'm sorry to hear that. I hope you recover soon."

June took a good look at the man, as he rambled on about the accident and how he had awakened with his leg amputated.

Oh, my goodness, It was the same Greg, who had ended their relationship so abruptly—two years ago to the day.

She introduced her husband to Greg.

Guillaume exuberantly added, "My wife and I are celebrating that we're pregnant with twins—a boy and a girl."

Greg looked sad, but offered congratulations.

They quickly said their good-byes.

It had rained while they were in the restaurant and June smiled as she noticed a double rainbow. She thought about what Guillaume had told her about what a double rainbow meant, when they first met.

June thought, *a double rainbow symbolizes a transformation in life—in my life.*

When in the car, June told Guillaume that Greg was the one who had broken her heart two years earlier.

Guillaume said, "Life goes on. I'm so glad that you

found love and happiness with me. June, I will love you and our babies for the rest of my life."

Guillaume kissed June with a deep passion and gently rubbed her tummy.

June knew in her heart of hearts that he meant every word.

She whispered, "I love you, mon mari chéri."

THE END

A NOTE TO READERS

You've finished the book. Thank you for taking the time to read my collection of short stories. Before you go, please take a moment to rate this book and leave a comment at the site from which you purchased this book. My only request is that you give me feedback.

MORE books by this author

Cougar Tales Series:

Father and Son (Book 1)
The Italian Basketball Player (Book 2)
Jamaican Love (Book 3)

Cougar Tales Series: Books 1-3 Box Set

The Bane Bath Salts (A drug prevention fiction eBook based on real-life events.)

The Proposal: A Leap of Faith (Short Story)

ABOUT THE AUTHOR

CHERYL HOLLOWAY is an award-winning writer, talk show host, journalist and retired writer-editor for the Federal Government. She has been the Editor of numerous Military magazines and newsletters; and was an intern at the Smithsonian Institution Press.

Cheryl is a dedicated writer, avid reader and amazing blogger. She won her first writing contest at 15-years old with a State Crime Prevention Essay in Indiana. She began writing feature articles and later became a sportswriter and Editor. This author and book lover also enjoys traveling to anyplace with a beach.

Cheryl is currently making her dream come true as an author. She lives in southern Maryland and northern California with her family, where she is hard at work on three other book projects that are works in progress.

You can email her at AuthorCherylHolloway@gmail.com or Check her website www.CherylHolloway.net for news, tours, book signings, awards or a book club in your area or visit her blog www.CherylHolloway.net/blog for writing tips and great book suggestions.

A CONVERSATION WITH CHERYL HOLLOWAY

1. **So, what makes *A Sisterhood of Women Living Life* special?**

   These are exciting stories taken from the lives of ordinary women. Some stories are honest, funny and heartfelt, while other stories are jam packed with deceit, betrayal and revenge. These stories are based on real-life events and I hope the readers will enjoy them and find them entertaining.

2. **The stories are about all kinds of women living life. Are these all stories from your life?**

   As you know, the stories are all based on real-life events. My experiences throughout life have provided materials for a plethora of short stories. However, some of the stories are from friends and people that I know and I embellished on the real-life event to create fictional stories.

3. **So, some of the characters are actually modeled from people you know?**

   Yes, bits and pieces of people that I know. I borrowed trivial details from various people and formed my characters.

4. **So, why should readers give this book a try?**

   These stories are for devoted romantics. They are real and relevant; yet, so true about the ups and downs of real-life love. Each story is a quick and easy read for today's busy women. And... she can boast about reading five short stories in one evening. She doesn't have to say that real short stories were only seven sentences long. LOL.

5. Do you enjoy writing romantic stories?

I have always enjoyed a good love story—especially, if I'm writing it. ☺ Seriously, whether the love story is in a book, such as *Like Water for Chocolate*, or *The Notebook*; or the love story is in a movie, such as *Doctor Zhivago*, *Les Parapluie de Cherbourg*, or *The Graduate*. Or whether the love story is in real life—my grandparents, who were married 53 years before my grandfather died; or my parents, who were married 46 years before my father died.

6. How long did it take you to write the book?

It took about a month to write and edit this book. There wasn't much research that I had to do. It took a little longer to finish the book, because of the feedback from the beta readers and the editor; and the formatting.

7. You have women of different ethnic backgrounds. Was this to make the book universal?

Yes, I wanted women of all ethnic groups and backgrounds, as well as all ages (18-50) to be able to read the book and to relate to someone like themselves.

8. Did you know how each short story would end when you started writing it?

No, because my characters seem to have a mind of their own once the story gets started and they take over the writing.

9. **Since this is Book 1, are there any plans for more books in the series?**

Yes, at the moment, I have started writing at least one other book in this series. There is a sneak preview of Book 2 with the short story, *June's Double Rainbow*. The next book may even have one story written from a male point of view.

10. **How did you start writing?**

You know the old cliché, "I've been writing for years." Actually, I have. Since I was about three years old, I used to write my own stories to add to my Golden Books library. I continued well into my teenage years, when I won a statewide essay writing contest on crime prevention at 15 years old. After majoring in Journalism at Indiana University, Bloomington, I became a technical writer for the Federal government and later a writer-editor for several newsletters and military magazines. Now, I'm a writer/author. So, I guess you can say that I've been a writer most of my life and I did fulfill my dream of becoming a writer.

11. **Do you have any other plans for the Sisterhood series?**

As a matter of fact, I do. I have a blog at:

http://www.CherylHolloway.net/blog.

On my blog, I had a Character Interview with Joi, from the Cougar Tales series, which was interesting and fun. Joi took over the interview and gave me her very lively opinions. Please check out the interview at:

http://www.cherylholloway.net/blog/2014/08/03/gu
est-character-interview-joi-from-cougar-tales/

So, I was thinking about doing a character interview with some of the reader's favorite characters from this book.

12. There are some really short stories included in this book. How did you decide to write these stories?

Well, I teach writing workshops from time-to-time. These stories are samples that I give my students for a writing exercise. I ask them to write a short story using only seven sentences. Each story must include a beginning, middle and ending. This has been a popular writing exercise and some good stories have evolved.

13. Is the book expensive?

No, not at all. You can purchase either the eBook or paperback on Amazon.com. Or my fans and supportive readers can actually email me for an autographed copy of the book.

14. What projects are you working on now?

I am currently working on a new romantic book with a dark side; however, I'm not quite ready to make the details public. All I can say is that once again, I am immersed in writing about characters, places, and situations that are unique. I'm also writing a couple of other books that I will make public real soon. You can visit my author page on Amazon to see all of my available books at:

http://amzn.to/1Rzsvxw

For more information about *A Sisterhood of Women Living Life: A Short Story Collection Book 1* or to order, please do one of the following:

- Visit http://www.Amazon.com/books

- Contact AuthorCherylHolloway@gmail.com

- Email Cheryl@CherylHollowayBooks.wordpress.com

- Visit my website at http://www.CherylHolloway.net

- Call us at 1-877-WRITE18

Do You Want To Follow Cheryl Holloway?

Subscribe to my blog for updates on new releases, epic giveaways, and books by other authors. Sign up today.

www.CherylHolloway.net/blog

You can follow me on:

Facebook:
https://www.facebook.com/cheryl.holloway.940

Twitter:
https://twitter.com/Author_CherylH

Email:
AuthorCherylHolloway@gmail.com

Now, you have all of the information, so have no reason not to follow me. You better get on it, right away, because I'm waiting to hear from you.

I know I'm lucky enough to have some real Super Fans, you know, the kind that would dive off a cliff for you. They have my back through and through. They love my books and they love spreading the word. Their biggest goal is wanting to see me on the New York Times or USA Today bestsellers list and they'll stop at nothing to make it happen. While it's a lot of work, it's also a lot of fun.

What better way to make friendships than to connect with people who love the same thing you do? Are you one of these super fans? If so, send a request to subscribe to my blog and if you want me to start a Facebook group for super fans, just email me to let me know.

Super Fans, book reviewers, bloggers; and newspaper and radio interviewers across the globe agree: "Cheryl Holloway is one of the most creative contemporary talents in America Today, and growing."

Thank you for reading!

To my Readers:

Thank you so much for taking time from your busy schedule to read one of my books or all of them. I deeply appreciate all of my readers—near and far—each and every one. Please remember to take a moment to rate the eBooks and print books and write a quick review on Amazon or Goodreads.

THANKS

Cheryl Holloway